Blades Falling Softly

A Novella of The Brightest Shadow

Version 1.0

© 2021 Sarah Lin

All rights reserved. This book or any portion thereof may not be reproduced or used in any manner whatsoever without the express written permission of the publisher except for the use of brief quotations in a book review.

Visit thebrightestshadow.blogspot.com for access to full resolution maps, concept art, and more!

Addendum

Attached to this letter is a troubling, oft-overlooked manuscript. The first several sections appear to be a simple manual of blade techniques and sein arts; well above average, but not truly remarkable. Yet as it progresses, it claims to record events that, if true, would be disturbing indeed.

The Taynol Valley is indeed a region in southwestern Nol, but given the toll of the conflict and subsequent riots, it is difficult to verify any of the claims made. One might be tempted to believe the manual is a fictional attempt to explain those events, except surely a mendacious author would not include such unbelievable claims. And if their attempt was to mock our Savior and Hero, why place those alleged secrets in an event of relatively little importance?

What I can confirm is that the two families named are real: Anyinn Tayn was accomplished enough to be placed in her clan's shrine, and there are records of someone named Canumon leaving the enemy military. For that reason, I include this manuscript despite my considerable doubts.

Anyinn

Every time Anyinn laid down her sword and picked up her quill, she found herself hesitating. The decisive strokes that came so easily in the courtyard abandoned her when she attempted to place them onto a scroll. All she had written so far covered only the humblest basics of what she hoped to leave for her descendants.

Her eyes wandered from the dried words to the activity in the courtyard beneath her. Just over the rail, students spun and twisted through the air, like leaves caught in the wind. They were children still drunk on their understanding of sein, leaping about in ways that would be suicidal in an actual battle, but they only brought a smile to her face. Still, to find anything worth writing, she would need to look onward.

The older students mostly trained beyond the first group, more reserved and more dangerous. Yet as Anyinn looked over their movements, she saw no insight that was worthy of inclusion. They were the steps and lunges that had been taught by her father and that she had taught to her children. If she wanted her manuscript to add anything to the legacy of the Tayn clan, she needed something new, something beyond the experiences of her own life.

Setting aside her quill, Anyinn gathered her robes around her and slid over the side of the balcony. She no longer saw or felt the rail and the marble floor - unchanged after so many years - only the landscape of the students around her. Though she could have named every one, they occupied a thin list in her mind, not the flood of memories from the previous generations she had trained.

Except the smallest of them, of course. Anyinn smiled as her gaze found its way to her daughter Heraenyas... at the same moment one of the students let out a cry of rage and pain.

Anyinn saw the student, a young man from a distant branch of the clan, pitching wildly toward a display of weapons. He had drawn deep on the sein within his soul, but without understanding or filtering it, leading to his own strength recoiling against him. It was clear that he would strike the weapons, jarring them from their places to scatter over the courtyard. She had more than enough time to intercept him, yet she found her hand flying to draw her sword, not to assist.

As the young man crashed into the display rack, Anyinn swept in faster than her students could blink. She pulled him back with one hand and grasped the rack with her other... but not quickly enough. Several of the blades flew from their places, directly toward Heraenyas. All the speed she'd spent a lifetime training gave her only the capacity to watch the blades flying toward her daughter, not to intercept them in time.

Yet Heraenyas leapt on instinct, hopping away from the weapons. In the next moment, the steel rang out against the wall, Anyinn swept up her daughter, and all the other students finally turned to look in shock.

Anyinn desperately wanted to hold Heraenyas tight, but she could already feel her squirming. Though she still saw the little girl dancing with flowers in her hair, she knew that her daughter no longer wanted to be treated as a child. Indeed, she'd just proved that she had begun to grasp the basics of her art.

So instead Anyinn set the girl down and turned to her students, her fear transmuted into anger that she struggled to swallow. By the time she reached the group, she had made her face calm, but all of them stared at her in apprehension. The boy most of all, already having dropped to one knee with his head lowered, so she spoke before he could begin an apology.

"How could this accident have been avoided?" she asked, her gaze meeting each student in turn before falling on the boy.

"I... I lost control of my sein." He stopped to swallow, only briefly managing to raise his eyes. "I was attempting... a technique too advanced for me."

"Perhaps." As Anyinn continued looking down at him, the simmering of her anger subsided. She thought of him as a boy, but that was only her age speaking: he was a young man, no doubt chafing at the limitations of the clan's teachings. "I heard not just pain in your voice, but anger. Why was that?"

"The power... it made me angry, and I started moving before I knew what I was doing."

"No." Anyinn knelt by the young man and grasped his shoulder firmly. "You have forgotten your earliest lessons. To think of sein as merely power is to forget yourself. Sein is everything that you are, and though that can be a great strength, it can also be a weakness. The flaw was not the technique you chose, but attempting to wield anger within you that you did not understand."

"Then...?" The young man finally dared to look up, hopeful, but she shook her head.

"Someone of your age should not be making such mistakes. I will send you back to your uncle for remedial training until he approves."

The emotions across his face were all so obvious: shock, indignation, shame, and eventual resignation. No doubt he thought this was the end of his life, humiliated in front of his peers and sent away - she remembered how such lessons had felt at his age. The fact that he lowered his head in acceptance instead of arguing spoke well of him, however, and he had many years to grow.

Though Anyinn gave the others a short lesson, her mind had already wandered on. As soon as she coaxed the atmosphere back to the peace of training, she turned to Heraenyas. Her daughter had her hands calmly tucked in her sleeves, an imitation of an adult, but she couldn't quite control her smile or keep herself from hopping back and forth.

"Mother... I did well, didn't I?" Heraenyas looked up at her with such undisguised eagerness that Anyinn couldn't help but smile in response. One day clan politics would teach her not to show her emotions so openly, but not yet.

"You were as swift as a waterfall, daughter. Not many with so little training could have avoided injury."

"I wanted to strike them!" A small hand shot out in a fist displaying more excitement than skill. "To knock all the weapons down just like you do! But... I jumped before I could think about it."

"And you did the right thing. Using your sein to move swiftly is a very different task from using it to block steel." Finally Anyinn reached out and touched her daughter's shoulders, caressing them affectionately. This, at least, the girl tolerated.

Sometimes it was difficult to believe that Heraenyas was her daughter, for all that they had the same dark hair and eyes. At that age, Anyinn had been shy and obedient, never even dreaming of something so aggressive as striking weapons out of the air. Yet her daughter threw herself into fights against children years older than her and eagerly pestered everyone she knew for stories of war.

It might have been the girl's nature, but Anyinn couldn't help but wonder if she had been responsible. The girl's two older brothers had both been far calmer children, clearly reflecting their parents. Their eldest had become the epitome of a Tayn warrior and though their second had left his sein training, he had become a responsible merchant philosopher.

Yet somehow, when she and Noreinu had decided to have one more child, they had produced Heraenyas. The girl had swept aside all of the phantasmal daughters that had once occupied Anyinn's mind.

With disaster averted, Anyinn gave her daughter a few suggestions and spent some time instructing her students on the finer points of sein. By the time she was done, she almost felt inspired to write something new, yet when she sat down, all her insights seemed pedestrian.

Before she could so much as wet her quill, the peace of the training chamber was disrupted once again: the doors slammed open and a young man strode inside.

She recognized Boulanu as one of the clan's independent warriors, usually traveling throughout the western forests. The fact that he had not come to train was obvious enough in his eyes and made undeniable by his combat robes and hat. Students went bareheaded as a matter of humility - though Anyinn suspected practicality played a larger role - but Boulanu wore a peaked hat at a rakish angle.

"Anyinn Tayn!" He must have seen her, but still made a show of looking over the students. "Enemies stand at our gates and the time for gentle instruction has passed! I challenge you for the position of school representative!"

"What are you doing, Boulanu?" Anyinn rose to her feet, keeping her hands within her sleeves to show she didn't acknowledge his challenge. "What enemies, and why do you believe you would better serve as our representative?"

"The fact that you don't even know what we face is another reason why you must step down! I have seen Deathspawn rising in the east and they will soon be upon us. Against such monsters, your Tranquil Blade will be meaningless."

Seeing that he would not back down so easily, Anyinn slowly walked to the marble floor, where a space rapidly cleared. She had heard tales of "Deathspawn monsters" but was not convinced they were anything more than human beings attempting to mask themselves in fierce legends. There were no more real Deathspawn in the world than there were winged lions or destined heroes.

When they met one another in the center of the marble diamond laid out for challenges, Anyinn lowered her voice to speak to her challenger alone. "Boulanu, are you certain you want to take this path? You must know how it will end. If you have concerns, you are always free to speak with me."

"You cannot stand against the strength I found in Nol Efeltalia! Stand aside, before they sweep us away!" Though Boulanu shouted, she caught an edge of fear in his voice. He took a deep breath and his sein swelled within him... vaster than before, but ill-considered. She doubted that he could even perceive his own soul with all his senses.

Like so many young warriors, he mistook force for strength. As the chimes rang to begin their match, Anyinn sighed. She had not wanted to humiliate him, but she could not ignore an official challenge from within the clan.

Like most careless warriors, his movements were all elaborate techniques and no footwork. No doubt he called his punch the Bull Rampaging Through the Forest, but his feet moved in a conspicuous line. Anyinn barely needed to call upon her sein to gently redirect his fist with the side of her sword.

Then she cast her free hand forward in the technique she had spent her life crafting: the Tranquil Blade. A sword appeared in his chest, formed not of steel but of memories. It shimmered so briefly it might not have existed at all, if not for the immediate undeniable effect.

Her opponent's eyes went distant as for an extended moment he lived her experience of resting beside a crystal lake, feeling nothing but contentment as she watched the leaves drift into the water through the dappled sunlight. She had forged the memory of that perfect day into a weapon that drew no blood and left no mark. Though his sein remained strong, only briefly overcome by hers, he slowly settled to the ground, his rage draining.

In return, Anyinn let his displaced sein stream through her. It was no concentrated experience, instead flashes of emotion and memory he had drawn on to attack her. More of the fragments were fear and concern than she had expected, driven by shuddering memories of threats. More rumor than substance, she thought, but she was surprised by how deeply he feared these supposed Deathspawn.

Some of her students began to whip their sleeves approvingly, but Anyinn silenced them with a glance. She bent down beside her fallen opponent, catching his gaze as he struggled to return to the present. He would find his rage again, so she considered a salve for his pride and spoke quietly.

"Now, speak clearly: what can you tell us of this threat we face?"

The tale that emerged was calm but fragmented: supposedly these Deathspawn had been attempting to infiltrate their lands through deals with Nolese merchants. It was unclear if this faction had a government or if they ignored the Nolese Coalition, but now they intended to invade the Taynol Valley by the ancient rites. Rumor had it that some so-called Deathspawn had already been spotted and that they would be forcing their claim within days.

As Anyinn settled back on her heels, her students scattered into rumor and gossip. The threat was not so illusory after all, if someone really did intend to invoke the Taynol Valley rites. But the very fact that they intended to claim ownership of unoccupied land through the traditional channels suggested that this was no invasion of monsters. Indeed, the rites could only be invoked by residents of Nol, so unless their claim was a pretext, she saw only clan politics in his story.

Yet it meant far more than that to her students, drunk on ancient tales of great wars. Seeing that no meaningful work would be done that day, Anyinn dismissed them with a futile command not to spread hearsay. As they dispersed, she carefully rolled up her manuscript, cleaned the training grounds, and finally locked the doors with the key around her neck.

By that time, only Heraenyas remained, eagerly miming strikes in the air. As they walked the long path back to their home, the girl jumped between rocks in a path of her own. Eventually even that was not enough outlet for her eagerness and she turned around to look at her.

"Mother, do you think the Deathspawn are really invading? Will there be war?"

"Perhaps there will be violence between clans, but I do not think it will be war." Or so Anyinn hoped, her mind falling back to the battlefields of the Efeltalian civil war. Even two decades past, those memories had teeth.

"But what if the monsters come? Are they really ten feet tall with burning eyes and lightning for hair?"

"That is a question for your father, I think. I have heard many tales of bizarre foreigners, but when I met them, they have all been humans of different shapes and colors."

Heraenyas sulked to the next rock, clearly having desired a better answer. She remained there as Anyinn caught up, then spoke in a lower voice. "Are you going to fight them? You're the strongest in the clan, right?"

"Not nearly." Anyinn chuckled as she bent to brush some of the wild hair from her daughter's face. "But as the school representative, I would be among those sent out if they invoke the rites. Whether or not there is any fighting will depend on the truth of these matters."

"Can I come?"

"I think you know the answer to that, don't you?"

Heaving a great sigh to indicate no one in clan history had ever been so unfairly treated, Heraenyas turned away and skipped ahead. Even her movements remained somewhat muted until they arrived home, unless that was Anyinn's thoughts coloring her world. As she grew older, sometimes she worried that she saw expectations and memories instead of what lay before her.

When they reached their home beside the cliff, Heraenyas ran in shouting of the day's events, and Anyinn smiled despite everything. She made her way to the door more slowly, seeing not so much the building as the events that had built it. Their sons begging to sleep on the roof as children, repairing the doorway as adolescents, walking out the gate to begin their own lives...

Though she moved as lightly as the wind, Anyinn's soul stumbled heavily by the time she entered. The sight of her husband bending down beside their daughter did much to warm her again. "You must be hungry after all that work," Noreinu said gently. "Why don't you wash up so that we can eat?"

"But Father..."

"I need to speak to Mother. You come back and join us." With that, he took off his artist's hat and flopped it down over her head. Heraenyas giggled like she never did in the school and tottered into the house half-blind.

As their daughter left, Noreinu rose to his feet and Anyinn was surprised how slowly and carefully he moved. When she looked at his face, she saw the river of their lives together more than his exact features, but she noted that his hair was grayer than she remembered. He had left his own sein training as a child, so the years weighed far heavier on him.

Anyinn took his hand as he rose and pulled closer to kiss his cheek. His hands were more lined than they had once been, but what she noticed was the paint staining them. "I see that you've been painting today."

"Poorly." He squeezed her hand and slid his other arm around her waist in a motion as practiced as any technique. "But I have no inspiration to write anything, so I made some feeble efforts at a canvas."

Though he was known as a playwright, Anyinn privately thought that her husband's painting was his greater skill, despite his protests. The dream-like brushstrokes might not be the current style in the Coalition courts, but she found them beautiful. Whereas she didn't doubt his skills as a writer, but all too often he stayed close to familiar war epics or the perennially popular romances.

"I wasn't able to write anything today either," Anyinn said as she put away her manuscript, "even before all the distractions. But I suppose Heraenyas has already told you the dramatic stories?"

"I think I might want another side of those stories." Noreinu chuckled and moved away to the small stove in the corner of the room. "Cup of neth?"

The familiar brewing process required no words, so Anyinn told her husband about the events of the day while they created the neth. Her husband was remarkably good at brewing neth, though her own sein was far better suited to heating than the fire. They kept two servants, a distant cousin and one of Anyinn's old students, but even they always insisted that the couple brew the tea themselves.

By the time they sat at the table with their cups, the recounting had lapsed into silence. Noreinu remained silent throughout, but now Anyinn caught his gaze and asked the question she had long held back. "Is there anything to these rumors of Deathspawn? Our valley is remote enough that few have seen anyone from Teralanth, or any barbarians from the Chorhan Expanse, so I always wondered..." Her words trailed off as she saw Noreinu shake his head.

"They are not human, Anyinn. They call themselves 'mansthein' instead of Deathspawn, but they are... on my last trip to Nol

Keralaln I saw several of them. Some might be mistaken for human from a distance, but... there is no question of it up close. There are others who appear even less human, hairless with mottled skin. And I heard rumors - credible rumors - that there are other clans and groups with monstrous size or beast-like claws."

Anyinn sighed and took a deep drink of the soothing neth. She could discount rumors from local warriors, but her husband was better traveled than she. "But they don't sound like monsters from children's stories."

"They sound like an empire, and that is bad enough." Noreinu set down his cup heavily and locked his gaze with hers. "They have fought wars in Fareshel and there are rumors that they might attack kingdoms in Eltar Trathe."

"Because they want what all empires want?"

"Who can say? But the Coalition believes that they will not attack us: the patchwork of clans across Nol is too formidable for them to fight. That's why they want to begin with trade and challenges. Boulanu may be a fool, but he *could* be right. Challenging via the rites could be a way for them to get a toehold in Nol, to steal what they can't win fairly."

She withheld her thoughts on the rumors of war: in her experience, every valley believed it had the strongest clans and every nation thought their warriors were more formidable than others. Her travels in Tur-Nol and the Chorhan Expanse led her to believe that every land possessed its own traditions of sein, each with something to recommend it. If these mansthein wanted to avoid war, it was more likely because their armies and greatest warriors were engaged on other fronts.

Since her husband had said nothing else, Anyinn decided to speak the inevitable conclusion. "So you believe that they truly do intend to force their way into the Taynol Valley."

"I can ask tomorrow, but I believe it's likely. We're in one of the few fertile parts of Nol where there's space for them to stake a claim. This could be the tip of the spear, Anyinn. If they send the representatives, it might fall on you to stop them."

"I will do what's necessary." She reached out to rub his hand and smiled, only for him to smile back wryly.

"But you hope 'what's necessary' is negotiation instead of violence, don't you?"

Anyinn only smiled again and returned to drinking her neth. She would do her duty, as she would against any human invaders who attempted to seize her clan's home. Hopefully that would be the end of it, yet the rumors of monsters worked their way beneath her skin, whispering promises that this time would be different than all previous challenges.

After the meal, Anyinn returned to her room and drifted into her own sein, reordering her soul with the familiar exercises. It left her calmer, but for once, she did not feel true peace. Soon enough, she would learn whether or not these invaders would change their lives.

Her practice left her with no grand insights to the arts of sein, yet when she sat down with her manuscript, Anyinn began to write.

Canumon

Though Canumon meant to meditate atop the hill, he found himself repeatedly hesitating. Part of his struggle was the strangeness of the wind on the hilltop, so different from his home in far eastern Nol. His mind also swarmed with thoughts of his wife, child, and quiet grief. It had been years since he'd been unable to master his own mind, yet he found himself distracted even by thoughts of food supplies and broken cabinets.

Of course, the armed warriors advancing toward his position were also relevant.

He had chosen this hilltop away from fertile lands because it was designated as a neutral place for anyone to train, not that he expected it to matter. Canumon slowly rose to his feet and saw the humans loping up the side of the hill like a pack of monkeys. All he could do was fold his arms in his sleeves as properly as possible and wait.

"Get out, Deathspawn!" The first of the men shook a club in his direction, as if he was an animal to be scared off. "You've invaded enough of our land!"

"I live in our town to the north and I have no intention of moving." Canumon had been speaking their tongue for twenty years, yet still found himself self-conscious of every inflection. As if it would matter. "This is no invasion."

"Just die!" A woman hurled a javelin at him and Canumon carefully stepped aside. His hands started to leave his sleeves and he considered defending himself, but restrained the impulse.

As a younger man, he would have fought them, demanding that they acknowledge his right to live in the land where he'd spent his entire adult life. When he looked back, Canumon had to admit that part of him was still repulsed: human bodies were covered in fine hairs and their eyes were always dull shades. If he had been able to interact with them, perhaps those feelings would have faded, but he'd just proved again that entering the space between their communities was an act of war.

Any revulsion faded before his second realization: they were all young and frightened. Human ages could be slightly difficult to determine, but he understood human sein, and most of the mob advancing on him were beginners. Only the leader was a real threat, his sein fully formed as if he had been training for ten years or more.

So Canumon simply stood and allowed the club to strike him across the face. Even gathering his sein against it, the blow hurt, sending him arcing off the side of the hill like a toy.

Canumon curled his shoulder as he hit the ground for the first time, blunting the impact without looking too adept. After bouncing again, he let himself skid through the grass and dirt before returning to his feet. In the distance, the humans shrieked victory and hatred at him, but they no longer attempted to pursue.

Faking a limp, Canumon slowly made his way back home. For the most part he was uninjured, though he found himself rubbing his jaw where the club had struck. That one was going to hurt. He felt the inside of his mouth with his tongue, noting how the point of one of his teeth shifted. Worrying at it with one hand, Canumon hoped that it wouldn't fall out.

He chuckled at himself, a warrior of his age and training nearly losing a tooth to a crude bludgeon. As a younger man, going through a rebirth focusing on the spiritual instead of the physical had seemed like the wisest of decisions, far wiser than his brutish peers. But of those peers who were still alive, he doubted they worried about losing teeth or aching backs.

Of course, had he been able to enter the rebirth chamber again, he could have mended those youthful mistakes. But he had about as much of a chance of that as jumping over the ocean, given the cost of a proper rebirth. Especially not with their funds going toward Gowanisa's medications.

As he walked, Canumon couldn't help but scan the landscape around him, despite the familiarity. It was an old habit from his military years, though these days his analysis was more social than tactical. As soon as the hills became slightly less rocky, they ceased being wilderness and he entered the mansthein side of the valley.

The lands of Nol were not cleanly divided between mansthein and human, instead forming a messy patchwork of old villages and recent military bases. To them, it was probably a Deathspawn stain on their nation. Until the generals back in Orphos had decided that Nol mattered, they had been restricted to the margins along the least desirable lands.

As he entered the outer periphery of the village, he witnessed yet again the brutal work required to survive in those borderlands. He passed herders first, moving their bovals from pasture to pasture, or rescuing the foolish creatures from obstacles. Beyond that came the fields, though only flavorless local grains could survive. Beside the town lay a small forest of trees, carefully tended to produce more of the fruits they naturally grew.

There had been a time when he'd hoped that the town would grow into the wastelands and they would begin intermixing with the human village on the other side. As much as humans liked to shout about Deathspawn, he thought that simple interaction and trade could have worn them down. But just hanging on to life here was difficult enough, for both sides, and if anything the hatred seemed to be intensifying.

Canumon rubbed his jaw again, pushing at his tooth from the outside. If he could have sat down with the old man who trained the human warriors, he thought that they could have come to an understanding. Surely their differences wouldn't matter so much, if they could speak long enough to reveal their similarities. Yet now it seemed he would never get that chance.

As he moved past the ramshackle houses of transient warriors to the stable center of the town, Canumon noted something new: a tent. And not just any tent, a vast canvas in the emerald of the Laenan military. Yet the mansthein he saw buying food nearby were Feinan, with self-supplied armor instead of the standardized kit of the Laenan military. That combined with the fact that they had shown up during the hours he'd been gone was more than a little strange.

Not that it had anything to do with him anymore. Canumon watched from the corner of his eyes to see if the soldiers would follow him, but they paid no attention and he returned the favor. That left him free to walk past them to the house.

It was nothing much, just wooden rafters above clay walls. The two rooms were enough for the pair of them and the baby, but it would be tight when Laghy grew up, especially if they managed to give him any siblings. Any that would be more than painful memories.

He let those thoughts run off him like rain and pushed through the doorway. Inside, he found Gowanisa lifting Laghy into the air as if he was jumping, the boy chortling at each leap and waving his arms aimlessly. His wife was covered in a sheen of sweat - she'd always been able to drop down and train in the most distracted of environments. For him, peace and solitude had been the bare minimum.

Gowanisa noticed the moment he entered, of course, and made their son reverse direction on the next leap. When he caught sight of Canumon, the boy shrieked "Ca!" and began flailing in his direction. With a fond smile, Gowanisa carried him in another jump into Canumon's arms. Once he held the boy, she wrapped her arms around him so their son was held between them.

"You're back early."

"It didn't go as smoothly as I'd hoped." His cheek must not have bruised yet, otherwise she would have understood. Canumon rubbed her back and leaned over their son's head to kiss her briefly. "Why are there soldiers in town?"

"They wouldn't tell me." Gowanisa drew back, smile fading as her attention shifted beyond their walls. "But there was a commander who wanted to talk to you, a Laenan man who said you'd served together. Do you know a Kanavakis?"

"Huh, maybe. Which faction is this group, if-"

"Ca!" Laghy headbutted his chest, disgruntled by the lack of attention. Canumon gave his wife an apologetic smile and pulled back to lift the boy into the air.

It seemed that he'd had enough of leaping games, however, instead grabbing at Canumon's hair with both hands. The boy liked to play with it, and seemed intent on shoving as much of it as possible into his mouth, but Canumon needed his hair, especially if he'd be meeting old comrades. He took Laghy down to his bed and gave the boy his finger instead.

Immediately Laghy latched on, pointy little nubs stabbing into his fingers. Their son had strong and even teeth, which was a blessing he thanked the Dark Lord for every day. Sometimes mixed blood between Laenan and Feinan led to snarled teeth, but so far the boy had grown up healthy.

Between bites, Laghy babbled on, imitating the way Canumon and Gowanisa spoke about their days. The sounds nearly brushed against words at times and Canumon responded attentively, wondering at how the noises tumbling like a stream would one day soon become real words. At the moment, the boy only used a few words coherently, or at least they'd only translated a few of his intentions.

With no warning whatsoever the boy went from frenetic energy to exhaustion and so Canumon tucked him into bed. Glad as he had been to see their son again, he needed time to talk to his wife. He had much to say about the confrontation at the hill, but when he emerged into the central room again, he spotted her by the stove.

That alone was nothing unusual, and the frying strips of boval meat were ordinary enough fare, but there was a steaming kettle on the stove. It wouldn't be neth, because his wife had always hated it, and there was a pungent odor that stirred memories...

"Is that...?" He stepped closer, reaching toward the kettle before pulling his hand back.

"I think I might be." Gowanisa didn't turn to face him, but when he embraced her from behind, she relaxed back against his chest. He slid a hand over her stomach even though he couldn't possibly feel the new life there.

"That's wonderful! Do you have enough herbs? I can make another trip to the city if you think it will be too long until the next market day. Wh-"

"Canumon." She turned around in his arms and dropped her head against his shoulder heavily. "I don't... I don't know if I want to feel hope this time. I'll do everything I can for the baby, but if we lose another..."

There was nothing he could say that had not already been said, so he only gripped his wife tighter. With their previous child, she hadn't even begun showing, so they had endured the loss alone. Not that the villagers would have understood, since most of them spawned violently without the herbs to manage a controlled pregnancy. Yet despite that pain, he still found hope swelling within him.

"Let me know what you need," he said finally. "We still have the money we put away from the match last year. I'll find something, do whatever I can."

"I know you will." When Gowanisa looked up at him, the pain in her smile mixed with other emotions. She leaned up to kiss him, this time more passionately, and Canumon slid his hand down to the small of her back.

A knock on the door. Both of them growled irritably.

There was no real choice, especially if it was who he expected. Canumon went to open the door and found himself face to face with Kanavakis. Canumon hadn't seen the man since he'd left the Laenan legions over two decades ago, but the commander hadn't changed much. His hair was grayer and his paunch larger, but he still had those steely red eyes.

"Laenan Canumon. Sorry to trouble you."

It had been a long time since he'd been called that, since the villagers didn't bother with titles, yet the old grammar returned quickly. "Kaen Kanavakis. If you're here for meat, I'm afraid we didn't prepare enough for an army."

Kanavakis chuckled, very briefly. "I need your fists, Canumon. Not to recruit you, not that again. But there's trouble with the humans further west and we need a civilian. Someone who can fight the way they do. I told them that if anyone could get along with these Nolese bastards, it was you."

"You came all this way for me?"

"Not just for you. It's more complicated than you know... the Senate is arguing over this again, but one of the Feinan factions sent an army. They're ostensibly under Laenan leadership, but how long will that last? So we need to move first, and move quickly. We don't need you to murder anyone, maybe just kill a few humans in fair duels. But if it doesn't work... well, you might need to leave anyway."

Canumon glanced over his shoulder at Gowanisa. She had poured herself a cup and held it steadily, but her fingers were very tight. "How certain is this?" Canumon asked.

"Everything's already in motion. We would need you to move to a place called the Taynol Valley and participate in an unknown number of duels. They'll start a damn war we can't afford, unless you can manage to get through to the humans. They're brutes, but the one thing their culture has is proper styles of combat. If you can fight well enough for them to respect you, this might not end badly."

"We... will think about it. We need time and more information."

"You need *time*?" Kanavakis looked over the tiny house with a barely disguised sneer. "This pissant little village isn't worthy of you, Canumon. If you do this for us, you'll be richly rewarded. You can still live in Nol and have a family. But this goes high... all the way to the top, do you understand me? This is the only moment that people like us can make a difference."

"We'll consider it." Canumon spoke with a friendly tone, but refused to look away from his former commander's gaze. "Wherever you're marching, you wouldn't have set up the tent if you were leaving tomorrow. There's time to think."

"But nothing to think about. Don't make a mistake, Canumon." With that, Kanavakis turned away and left them alone again, though now Canumon couldn't ignore the sounds of the soldiers bartering outside.

At least their visitor hadn't woken Laghy, but in his absence the home felt wrong, as if it tilted violently to the side. Gowanisa finished her herbal drink but didn't say anything, just staring at him. Despite the abruptness of it, Canumon realized that he was seriously considering the offer.

"Do you know anything about this Taynol Valley?" he asked. "If it isn't far, we might not have to give up the house. I know it's sudden, but offers like this... they're not meant to be refused."

"I should have torn out his throat when he came in the first time." His wife set her cup on the stove, her claws raking the metal as they pulled away. "But you're right, there's not much of a choice. Apparently you need to kill some humans or our lives will be ruined anyway."

"If it's to the west, we'd be deep in human territory. Do you think that you can find the right herbs there? We'd be nearer Nol Efeltalia, and I know there's some mansthein shipping there, but I don't know if it would be practical."

"That's the wrong question." She came over to stand beside him, staring at the closed door. "They don't need strength for this, they need you. That means they're using us. It might be true that they can't afford a war right now, but how far do you think they'd go for peace? Not this far. I don't like that we don't know what they want."

"Neither do I, but..." Canumon reached around her waist again, this time just lashing the two of them together. "Does that mean we're considering this?"

"I don't think we have a choice."

Anyinn

The bluff loomed at the northern end of the Taynol Valley, a gargantuan tortoise fallen asleep amid the fertile hills. Over the course of her life, Anyinn had fought rites there three different times, losing as an adolescent but winning both rites as clan representative. Despite the tension, all three duels had been surprisingly peaceful, a sober contest of skills to resolve a conflict.

As soon as her escort brought her within sight, she knew that this time would not be so simple.

One of the vast stones at the base of the bluff lay sundered, a body lying in the newborn crevice. Anyinn could see the blood staining the man's combat robes, but he had sold his life dearly: two bodies crumpled nearby. Above them, she saw several fighters exchanging stances on the path upward and two more atop the bluff.

"This isn't..." The young woman who had escorted her stared in shock, eyes struggling to follow the rapid movements. "The rites were meant to start at noon... how can they have...?"

"You've fulfilled your duties by bringing me here." Anyinn gave the escort an encouraging smile and gestured back to their path. "Return and tell them that someone has disrupted the rites, and we must determine who before we leap to conclusions."

Thankfully, the young woman kept her head and hurried back. The primary goal was to take her away from the danger, but if she was able to bring reinforcements with order on their minds instead of revenge, that would be better. Anyinn drew her sword but held it at her side as she approached, resolved to understand the conflict before she struck.

The dead man was indeed Nolese, his hair a familiar blond-black, but the bodies around him seized her attention. They could only be mansthein: their skin was a mottled orange she had never seen in humans, the blankly staring eyes were crimson, and their hands ended in short claws. She could have overlooked accidents of coloration, but she found herself fixating on the sides of their heads: instead of ears, they had only protruding ridges of bone. It was easy to imagine how young warriors could mistake them for legendary Deathspawn.

But these fallen corpses looked like nothing but casualties to her. Perhaps they had betrayed the terms of the rite, but they might also be victims. As Anyinn gathered her sein to prepare to leap, she let her eyes slide over the bluff to find the point where she could be of the most use.

And the first thing she saw was another Deathspawn, crouched like an animal with his teeth dripping blood. He had struck down a Nolese warrior and apparently torn into his neck. Despite her desire for restraint, Anyinn felt a surging impulse to strike him down before he could savage anyone else.

She floated to their position on her own memories and saw the mansthein turn toward her in alarm. His rising fist was far too slow, sliding through the air so lazily that she had time to check her impulse to run him through and instead gather a blade of pure sein.

When the Tranquil Blade struck him he had no defense and slumped to the ground, overwhelmed by the serenity of her sein, but Anyinn was struck by the uncontrolled explosion from his soul. His sein was a flood of his most recent memories, fragments of a desperate battle with the man fallen beside him. She felt an echo of the intense pain in her arm and the desperation that led her to sink her teeth into her opponent's neck.

Anyinn wavered, her tongue tasting blood even though her mouth was clear. She was in no danger, her opponent thoroughly stilled, but she was no longer certain what to do. Even if he was more than a savage beast, his hatred and intent to kill had been clear as well. Looking down, she realized that his opponent still lived, gripping his neck to limit the blood loss.

Before she could decide, she heard a terrible crack of stone meeting bodies that were yet more durable. When she looked toward the source, she saw that the duel atop the bluff had broken off a large fragment of rock that now rumbled down the slope toward them.

Even she had little time to act, so Anyinn swiftly picked up the fallen man, not hesitating when she realized that she was leaving the stunned mansthein to die. It was a poor decision, but if she could save only one life, her own people came first.

Another mansthein skidded down the side of the hill, faster even than the tumbling stones. Anyinn braced herself to evade, but aside from a glance in her direction, he ignored her, instead scooping up the fallen mansthein and leaping from the avalanche.

Their robes fluttered around them as they leapt to a safe distance, eyes partially on the rocks as they crashed to the ground and mostly watching one another. Judging from his ease of movement, the mansthein could have taken the opportunity to attack her, but chose not to. After a wary glance, they retreated to set down their injured warriors, and she used that moment to observe him more carefully.

Unlike the other mansthein, he had short dark hair that could have been Nolese if not for the greenish tint. Skin lighter than others she'd seen and striped instead of mottled. Thin horns ran back from his head in the same line as his hair. His robes, as yet untouched, might actually have been Nolese linen, even if the cut was no clan she knew. Instead of bone ridges, oddly elongated ears lay flat against his head. Seeing him, Anyinn understood what her husband had said about mistaking some mansthein for human... but his eyes glowed an infernal crimson far worse than that of the corpse or the savage.

"We did not strike first." The mansthein warrior spoke in clear Nolese, though with an eastern accent. He turned toward her without aggression, setting his feet carefully. "This was meant to be a peaceful rite of combat and we were set upon."

"If that is true, you deserve our apologies." Anyinn kept her sword at her side. "But you will forgive me if I do not accept your word without evidence. Will you wait for the authorities to arrive and determine the truth of what happened here?"

"What reason do I have to believe that they won't exterminate me as soon as they arrive, as the others tried to do?"

"You have my word. If you are innocent, I will prevent them from laying a hand on you."

"With all due respect, I'm not sure either of us is in control here." And as he spoke, he smiled, and all of Anyinn's intuitions came tumbling down.

It had been decades since interpreting the expressions of others had been anything other than effortless, yet now her second nature led her wrong. The mansthein's smile didn't part his lips, but the muscles beside his eyes did shift. Yet their pattern was subtly different and she had no way of knowing if that was due to his nature or if it threatened deceit.

"Then I see no alternative." Anyinn raised her sword at shoulder height to point toward his heart. "Why did you come here?"

"To engage in the rites and earn a place in the Taynol Valley for my family, with the strength of my own hands."

He knew the words, and she wanted to believe him, but Anyinn kept her expression neutral. "Then as a representative of the Tayn clan, it is my duty to meet your challenge."

Though he might have looked disappointed for a single heartbeat, the mansthein soon raised his hands in front of him and shifted his stance. Their first exchange of blows passed so swiftly that she reacted on pure instinct, and though Anyinn soon regained her calm, she found herself smiling.

His footwork reminded her of the Circling Leviathan stance, though it was a crude imitation. Despite that, he had the strength to meet her blade with his bare hands and the speed to neutralize the greater reach of her sword. Unlike so many young warriors, who sought to batter down their opponents with greater sein, he understood himself deeply.

Yet as they exchanged techniques again, she saw that he couldn't overcome the flaws in his training. Since he had been so civil, Anyinn had no intention of killing him, but knew that as a sein-trained warrior he could survive a direct blow from a sword.

At last she saw another flaw and thrust forward, her blade a glimmer of sunlight... an inadequate glimmer. Her opponent evaded the thrust in a twisting moment that would never have been used from Circling Leviathan, then struck out with a blow more akin to Punishing Willow.

She managed to evade his palm, but the momentum sent her sliding over the grasses, barely remaining on her feet. A younger warrior might have been bested in that moment, but Anyinn had faced more than a few surprises in her time. When he pursued her, she kept him at bay with Waterfall Cascading Upward and regained her footing to match him.

With each exchange, she realized that she had misjudged him. His stance was not a crude version of Circling Leviathan, but a polished art unfamiliar to her. Realizing that her own assumptions would lead to her defeat, Anyinn resolved to end their duel in the next exchange.

For that, there was only one technique: she raised her free hand and drove the Tranquil Blade into his heart.

Yet to her shock, the mansthein caught the thrust between his palms. The blade was nothing but a shimmering fragment of sein, yet he managed to intercept a spiritual presence. While her mind recoiled, her training automatically pushed forward, finally piercing him with her technique.

This time, the sein flooded into her beyond her control. Anyinn at first flinched at the memory of a monstrous woman, yet the sein carried with it so much warmth that she was caught up in her opponent's mind. In a moment, she found herself falling into images of a loving wife and a laughing baby, a scene of such overwhelming domesticity that she stumbled backward.

When the connection ended, Anyinn emerged taking deep breaths, trying to ready herself if he intended to attack her. Yet her opponent stood still, the expression of peace on his face mixed with a longing that she couldn't understand. He turned toward her with a pained smile that still rang false to her, yet after experiencing those emotions...

"I have enjoyed dueling you... but I do not want it to continue like this."

"I agree." Anyinn straightened her spine and sheathed her blade, finally allowing herself to smile at him. "I struggle to believe that you comprehended my technique and reacted so quickly."

"Ah, you do me too much credit." As the peace faded, he shook his head ruefully. "It is a formidable technique and I could never have countered on my own. I was fortunate enough to see you perform it before, on my ally there."

So he had seen her blade of sein once, from across a battlefield, while leaping down the side of a bluff. In another man's mouth, she would have thought the humility only another boast, yet she found herself believing him. Though it might only have been the feel of his sein - which she reminded herself was an intentional counter he might have used to deceive her - she didn't think he meant anything but respect.

"If you are to be my opponent," he said, "I suppose that it will not be so easy to earn our place in this valley."

"That was your family?" Though she asked the question, the look in his eyes was all the answer she needed, so Anyinn shook her head. "I don't think it will be allowed, no matter your skill... what you said about being attacked first was true?"

"It was. I don't know if it was a moment of anger or if this was planned as an ambush from the start, but one of your warriors killed one of ours without warning."

"If that is so..." Anyinn turned away and began thoroughly inspecting a patch of ground. "Perhaps it would be best if you evaded me and escaped, despite my best efforts."

She thought that she saw him grin from the corner of her eyes, but not well enough to know if the expression was authentic. Even if she had been able to see his face, it would only have been a mixture of alien and familiar that she couldn't read. So Anyinn remained focused away for several heartbeats longer until she felt his presence diminish.

Her anonymous opponent had taken the injured mansthein with him and it looked as though the others had retreated. Remembering her own fallen ally, Anyinn knelt to bandage his wound. His sein was strong, so he would live, but if properly cared for he might be able to avoid a lingering injury or even a scar.

As she worked, Anyinn found herself staring past the bluff, at no one.

Canumon

"This one came close." Gowanisa held up his combat robes in one hand, poking a claw into the cut. "A little slower and she might have torn open your guts. Was it really that close?"

"I don't even remember that as a close call, to be honest with you." From his seated position, Canumon continued to mend another of the cuts to his outer robe. "She was so fast that staying far away was a luxury I couldn't afford. I had to stay on the edge the entire time or I would have lost."

Gowanisa snorted. "Then fighting her up close is lunacy. I've always said that you need to be better fighting at range."

"Maybe so." The apparent scorn was just her concern for him spilling over, so Canumon nodded without arguing. Besides, she was right. If he could have had his life to live again, he would have focused on different techniques to make himself more flexible. But he was an old man and his deep knowledge of his own sein left it rigid as a building's foundation.

As he continued repairing his robes, Canumon couldn't help but look around the room yet again. Even though there was no threat and he knew the floor plan by heart, he felt uncertain outside of their familiar home. Tent walls were less secure as well, giving little warning if someone attempted to attack through them.

Still, he had to admit that the army had placed them comfortably. This tent was nothing like the draped tarps he remembered from the military, instead an elaborate construction that had required several soldiers to raise. Divided into three different chambers, it was actually more spacious than their original home. Chairs and cabinets had been provided for them, workmanlike but in better repair than what they'd owned before. There was even a cradle for Laghy.

It wasn't home, though. And given how the fight had gone, he wasn't certain that he could earn one.

"What if..." Gowanisa hesitated as she set down his robe, just staring at him. "If we fought her together, do you think we could win?"

"I'm not sure." It wasn't quite honest and her eyes narrowed, so he pressed on. "We were evenly matched, so with you striking at range, she might be overwhelmed. But she was very experienced... I think she'd likely turn on you, and I don't know that we could counter effectively."

That rubbed up against sore subjects, but to his surprise, his wife just shook her head. "Be careful." She moved to embrace him and ran her claws gently over the muscles of his back. "I want to go along next time, just in case it's another ambush."

"I hope that it won't be. She had a sense of honor, I think."

"But still. Is it worth the risk?" One of Gowanisa's hands slid down to her stomach and he knew that she was contemplating every one of the risks. All he could do was hold her tighter.

They barely had a few heartbeats together before a loud cough interrupted them and then Kanavakis pushed through the tent flap. Despite the circumstances, he was grinning, trying and failing not to show his teeth. Gowanisa immediately pulled back and handed Canumon his repaired robe, remaining in the door of the next room.

"I knew I was right to pick you, you old bastard." Kanavakis saluted him as if he was still a subordinate. "I thought it might go to hell, but apparently you made an impact on one of the humans. They spoke up for our version of events and none of the clans are going to war. If you hadn't earned their respect, there would be fighting already."

Canumon sighed and didn't return the salute. "Our version of events is the real version."

"That may be true, but it doesn't really matter, does it? All that matters is the story people tell about it: and right now, everybody is still talking treachery. On both sides. We need to do a proper human rite and we need to do it soon. Or maybe an even quicker duel, before things boil over."

"Just what is boiling?"

"The main army, of course. The veterans might be happy to let the real warriors fight, but most of this group is unblooded idiots straight from Fein Karnak. How long do you think a bunch of Feinans can be trusted to stay civilized?" Kanavakis belatedly glanced at Gowanisa and tapped his cap. "No offense intended, Naena."

"How could I possibly take offense, Kaen Laenan?" Gowanisa spat the words like acid and then turned away, though she would still be listening closely. Since the two of them would never get along, Canumon decided to stand up and face the issue head on.

"So you intend to set up another combat rite as soon as possible?" he asked. "Are you sure it won't be another ambush?"

"The official human line is that one of their warriors just wanted to start the battle and it was only our weakness that led to a death." Kanavakis snorted and shook his head. "I told you, they only respect strength, and only on their own terms. There was another clan, where we tried to send Catai... we won, but the humans didn't respect it."

Canumon frowned. "This has been tried before? What happened?"

"That's more than you need to know, Nin Canumon. What we need you to do is sign an official challenge, as soon as we can get the details worked out. Then win, or at least fight well enough that the humans will treat fairly with us."

"Who would I be fighting against?"

"I told you, we need to work out the details. But we wanted to start with a challenge according to their customs, so I need your signature today."

Though Kanavakis pulled a piece of parchment from his bag and set it down on the table, Canumon remained where he stood, considering. Part of him deeply wanted to fight the human woman again. Their blows had reached one another even in the midst of the bloodshed: if they fought without anger, how much more might they learn from each other? But Kanavakis already had quill and ink ready, eager to draw him into the broader scheme.

So Canumon took the quill, but only held it in both hands as he spoke. "If you want me to do this for you, I need more than promises of money. I need you to explain why they're pushing for all of this."

"You really need to know? You think that they tell me everything?"

"I think that you need me, now that I'm your link to the human warrior clans."

Kanavakis glowered at him, eyes burning, but after grinding his teeth for a while, he did answer. "It's politics, so there's more than one reason. Some want the Nolese Coalition to acknowledge us so that they can move more goods through Nol Keralaln without being robbed by excessive tariffs."

"For a war in Eltar Trathe?"

"Moneylust comes first, I think, but maybe bloodlust later. There's talk about shipping routes to Tur-Nol and maybe even further west. The Senate has interest in the Reynt Islands, but going directly across the Exantic Ocean without a stopover is just too far. Is that enough for you? Do you need me to go over every item in the merchants' agenda line by line?"

Though Canumon thought that what he'd been told so far had the ring of truth, he knew that couldn't be all. Yet his position wasn't so strong that he could keep pushing, so he considered his last question carefully. "Why the Taynol Valley? This is a nice enough land, but it's not essential to anything. I refuse to believe you couldn't find any other clan with rites of entrance."

Again Kanavakis ground his teeth, but this time it looked more like apprehension. "This is... some parts of this go to the top. Someone powerful thinks that mining rights in the region will be essential, and they want to gain them without a war against the humans. But that's really all I know."

"Mining rights?" Canumon knew that the mansthein war machine was desperate for metals, precious or violent, but he doubted the mines of one valley could be so important. There was no way to find answers and Kanavakis had reached the limits of his patience, so after turning the matter over in his head and glancing at Gowanisa, Canumon nodded.

Dipping the quill into the ink, he signed the right side of the official challenge. The language was vague, but it didn't commit him to anything extreme. He'd automatically signed his name in Nolese characters, but after a moment of thought, wrote his name in Futhik as well. Contrary to what Kanavakis believed about Nolese, Canumon thought they might appreciate the artistry of it. He might not be a master calligrapher, but the formal challenge would defy those who expected a clawprint.

As soon as he had his parchment, Kanavakis swept away with few more words. That was all he needed from them, after all. Canumon expected to be treated fairly, so he tried to focus on the final payment and the possibility of a new, permanent home... instead of the likely complications and the potential consequences beyond his sight.

Once Kanavakis was gone, Gowanisa emerged again. "Even if he means well, this isn't a military operation, it's politics." She grimaced toward the tent flap as if she could still smell him. "Try to win this fight, Canumon. Get us out of it quickly, before everything turns ugly."

"I wasn't planning on surrendering." He put an arm around her waist to take any sting from the words, but just as she began to lean her head against his shoulder, they were interrupted by Laghy's cries.

Both of them went to the small room with the cradle, and as soon as their son saw them, he gurgled and clapped his claws together gleefully. Canumon had heard endless tales of how miserable children could be, yet Laghy's mood was almost perpetually happy. When he bent over to tease at his son's teeth, however, the boy spat out his finger.

"No! Oma! Oma!" Laghy stretched his claws toward Gowanisa, and when she picked him up, the boy tugged at her shirt. Gowanisa had nursed him just before his nap and now hesitated.

"Do you think we should keep giving him milk?" She looked toward Canumon, though it was really a question for herself. "He should be eating meat soon, or his teeth will go bad. The boy needs to grow up sometime."

"Does it have to be now?" Canumon asked. "Do we want it to be?"

His wife sighed and held the squirming baby closer. "It can be a little longer."

Anyinn

There had been a time when Anyinn leaving for battle had been a more dramatic affair: whispered promises, tangled sheets, desperate fears. Though the danger was no less than many past challenges, the years had filed off the edges of their concern.

Now, they simply walked together, away from civilized hills toward the Lonely Diamond. Her husband had insisted on accompanying her this far, but in the end it would be unwise for him to leave the Taynol Valley. The probability of another clan, or some faction of mansthein, attempting to strike at them and pretend it was an accident was simply too high.

"I suppose you want to run the rest of the way now." Noreinu spoke quietly, without any hidden dissatisfaction, merely trying to judge the distance. Anyinn reached out to take her husband's hand, stopping his steps so she could interlace their fingers.

"We have a little time yet, before the rite. But we've walked far enough that the distance will make no real difference."

"I'd prefer to walk, just to clear my mind." He began to move forward again, though he kept her hand in his. "I trust you to fight this duel as well as it can be fought, but please remember the aftermath. What story they tell about today will set the tone for the full rite."

"What story are they already telling?" Though Anyinn thought that she could be trusted to know her business, if her husband was concerned, it must be even more complex than she knew.

"Some think you're very brave, standing for Nol against the Deathspawn menace. Others are calling the entire clan naive to even grant them a duel. And a great many think that the mansthein are targeting the warrior clans to avoid the politicians, our strength becoming weakness."

"And they think that ignoring or refusing the challenge would serve us better? It's not a matter of pride, it's a matter of Nol's reputation."

"Stories don't have to be true to matter." A smile played on Noreinu's face as he glanced toward her and finally held her gaze. "I wish I had some insight for you, but no one knows what this story will be yet. All I can do is ask you to be careful."

She squeezed his hand tighter and smiled back. "I will. But usually, a few local duels aren't cause for any stories at all. Has ours gathered so much attention so quickly?"

"It's more than a challenge." His smile gave way to an expression of blank thought she associated with his writing moods, yet something hard and cold lurked in the blankness. "You know the legend about the Deathspawn? Their 'Dark Lord' and the battle before the end of the world?"

"You're being rhetorical, dear husband."

"Sorry. But I honestly hadn't thought about it for years, not even as an allusion in a script. It's too... grandiose, too downright old-fashioned. Yet there are others talking about this conflict in mythic terms. Men and women I respect treating this as something far more than it is and expecting bloodshed. I half-expect them to begin begging for the arrival of a mystical hero to carry us to victory."

Then that uncertainty, that loss of his peers, was what lay beneath his concern. Anyinn had never felt his impulse to create, but this time her sword would serve as quill. She stopped, took his hand in both of hers, and kissed it softly. "Let them talk, Noreinu. There will always be swirling rumors, but true artists can shift the tide. And perhaps this time you can write me into one of your little dramas."

He smiled wryly and squeezed her hand one more time before he let go. Feeble as they were, her words did seem to have reached him, perhaps because she believed them: the discussion had been dominated by fear and uncertainty, but she thought the battle that day would bring great clarity. Once that had been achieved, she and her husband could set about redefining the stories told of these duels.

They could have said farewell, but they had long ago agreed to leave some words unsaid. Anyinn turned away and at last began to run, the landscape melting beneath her. Caught in the grip of her sein, her body moved far faster than any untrained runner or beast, taking her from the outskirts of her valley into the rocky wilderness.

As a younger woman it might have taken her more time and she would have been able to think about the match, but all too soon she found herself reaching the Lonely Diamond. She slowed down to examine the region more carefully: several mansthein representatives stood at a distance, but they didn't appear to be sein-trained. Other than them, only her opponent stood atop the marble, his hands in his sleeves, a statue woken only by her challenge.

Anyinn smiled on unconsidered instinct but made her expression sober before she slowed to a halt atop the marble. Her mansthein opponent straightened and looked at her, but the space between them became suddenly awkward. The tension of combat had been far easier than this uncertain social framing and she nearly decided to attack him to ease it when he finally spoke.

"They called this place the Lonely Diamond. I understand why it is lonely, but why build so far away?"

She hesitated, for the first time considering how the familiar landscape might appear to fresh eyes. The Lonely Diamond was an inscribed piece of dark marble with stairs cut into two of the points for the contestants to enter. All along the sides sprawled carved glyphs that looked similar to the modern Nolese script but to Anyinn's knowledge had never been translated. Broken flagstones marred the landscape around it, along with the remnants of several small towers that had not endured as well as the Diamond itself.

"We do not know the true name of this place," Anyinn said, lapsing into her instructor's voice as she gestured to the ruins. "Several clans claim to have founded it, but there are no clear records. Generations past, this was fertile land and many clans fought rites and duels here. Now that it lies in the wilderness, it has often been used as a neutral location for meetings."

"Like ours."

"Yes, I suppose so." She lowered her hand to rest on the hilt of her sword but maintained a neutral stance. "You wrote your name on the challenge, but this has all been done so formally... perhaps we should introduce ourselves."

"My name is Canumon, clanless by your standards, but of the Laenan mansthein." He bowed respectfully and pulled his hands from his sleeves. "I seek a rite of challenge for myself and my family to enter your valley and call it home."

"I am Anyinn Tayn, representative of my school and of the Tayn clan. We do not grant you a duel with residence in the valley at stake, but instead a trial. If you prove yourself worthy against me, your challenge will be conducted in a true rite."

Everything they said was rote, modified only slightly by the unusual circumstances, but it calmed her to repeat the familiar words. Perhaps her husband had been right and it would have been better to bring others from the clan to witness, as she had no idea what the mansthein observers thought. None of them were dressed in Nolese robes, so she could only imagine the social connections between them.

Her idle thoughts fell away as her opponent - Canumon Laenan - stepped forward and they resumed their dance.

Canumon

As Tayn Anyinn drew her sword, Canumon should have prepared for the fight of his life. He knew his opponent's strength, and on his path to the duel, everyone had reminded him how much was at stake. Even winning was no guarantee of success, not with so many eyes on them.

Instead of preparing, he smiled.

They met in an exchange that mirrored the previous day, essentially just a reintroduction now that they had given their names. When he had been younger, combat had been a rush of passion and panic, but that had changed as his sein deepened. Moving beyond the speed of the wind and enduring direct blows removed the fear and opened the possibility of play.

Tayn Anyinn was an able partner in that game. It was clear in every stroke that she was a swordswoman accustomed to training with martial artists, making no attempts at superficial cuts that would glance off. Yet she wove an elegant defense that threatened a far deeper strike if he advanced too far, and each thrust forced him into desperate evasions.

Her language of combat was clearly based on formal techniques and he could see her categorizing each of his movements and selecting the proper response. Yet she was not limited to a rigid formula, instead moving like a dancer who knew the steps and also when to leave them.

Their graceful exchanges ended in a sudden moment of pain as their defenses broke: her sword cut his side and his palm struck her arm.

Canumon dropped back, gripping the injury. It bled profusely into his robes, but wasn't so deep. He took a deep breath and let his sein curl and blossom at his side, sustaining the injured flesh so that he could continue. Anyinn performed an artful trick over her arm and flexed it cautiously, but she didn't strike as he knew she could.

"This fight or the next would prove little," the human woman said. "In the end one of us would die and nothing would be proved. I propose an alternative: let each of us put forward our greatest student. The test of our ability to teach would be a better judge of our true skill."

"Like in the ballads?" Canumon recognized the familiar allusion, but it did him no good at all. This was clearly a concession, an invitation to the Nolese martial community, and he could not respond. "I'm afraid that I have no students, past or present."

He saw a flicker of surprise on her face, more than she'd ever displayed at any of his techniques. Most likely he knew what she was thinking. The veneration of teaching was an uncommon attitude among most mansthein, but he'd become familiar with it in the Nolese community.

"Can that be true?" She pointed her sword in his direction, still stained with his blood, but her strike was solely verbal. "Before today, I would have said that it was impossible to gain a real understanding of sein without having taught it. Even the most isolated of masters have taken on students to advance their own progress."

"In my experience," Canumon said slowly, "those who teach sein are so confident that they already know everything that they never understand themselves."

Anyinn sniffed. "You seem very confident in that perspective."

"Not so much. Perhaps both of us should admit that we are middling old warriors. If we had any idea what we were talking about, we would be true masters instead of squabbling with one another over definitions." Taking that approach was a risk and Canumon held his breath. After staring at him with that unreadable expression, Anyinn's face suddenly broke into a human smile.

"Perhaps you're right." She cleaned off her sword on the edge of her robe but kept it at her side. "Then please be patient with an old woman who needs time to recover. Tell me, why have you studied our culture in such depth?"

"I was born on Orphos, but I came to Nol as a very young man. I've lived here most of my life, and Nolese comes to me quicker than Futhik." Not always true, considering how long he'd spent in mansthein communities, but enough of a truth to offer. "To the east, there are more of us than you might think, but we live in the borderlands where the Nolese Coalition doesn't maintain order."

"And so now you seek to challenge your way into the Taynol Valley."

"Something like that. I'm getting older, and my family needs a home where we can rest."

Her sword stabbed out at him, her words just like the thrust. "Don't lie to me. If you tell me that you simply decided to come to my home, with no influence from outsiders, then I will be very disappointed by your lies."

"I said we needed a home, not that nothing else motivated my decision." Canumon raised one hand with fingers extended, half-way between a defensive stance and a rhetorical pose. "Your rites of challenge say that any warrior of Nol can earn their right to a home by proving their strength. I'm sure that those rites have never held any political meaning whatsoever, among humans."

"It is not the same thing, and you know it. The mansthein who sent you intend to use our rites against us."

"You're right, it's not the same thing." Canumon knew that he should control himself, but let the words spill out like a series of blows. "The words of the rite are the lie: you claim that anyone can step forward, but you mean only humans. Your people have fought one another for generations, but when a foreigner tries to join you, suddenly the rites no longer apply! How many humans have you rejected because they have ulterior motives?"

Though Anyinn took a step back and lowered her sword, she took only a moment to regroup. "You may have a point, but that point only goes so far. Can you look me in the eye and tell me that your military isn't using you to gain access to my home?"

Such a swift counter, driving at the greatest weakness in his armor. Canumon suffocated an impulse to be honest with her and express his own concerns honestly. That might appeal now, but he was fighting this battle for Gowanisa and Laghy. If he wanted a future in which they could live in the Taynol Valley without war, he needed to choose his words carefully.

"You already know there is an army on your doorstep. If it wanted to force a claim, it could." Despite his consideration, he regretted his words almost immediately and stepped back. "All we want is what any other group could claim: trade and training and mutual betterment. The army is nothing but protection in case our claim is denied and you seek to wipe us out."

"Or a threat. A sword at the side can cut deeper than a sword in the hand." Anyinn regarded him somberly, dull human eyes piercing. "I wish that I could believe you, but you know your empire's reputation. I cannot know if you are a deceiver or a fool."

"Then let me show you what I am."

Canumon dropped into a full fighting stance and took a step forward. He saw the disapproving flicker in Anyinn's eyes and she lowered her sword, prepared to defend herself. In that moment she could have struck and renewed the violence between them, but he moved first.

Instead of a true attack, he stepped forward in exactly the same technique that had begun their first fight beside the bluff. She automatically countered as she had before... and he followed with the movement he had then, as if they were following a script.

Step by step, they retraced their techniques. Canumon saw the suspicion in her eyes, waiting for the moment where he would break the pattern to strike her, but he walked it like a paved path. Gradually their movements became smoother, the formalized ritual of two allies in a single school. It was a moment of peace that would not be sufficient, but it would end in the brilliant technique he had seen before.

Just as he had hoped, she manifested the shimmering blade that slid into his heart with deceptive simplicity. Even as he countered, he took a deep breath and welcomed it.

The momentary experience captivated him in a way that sein rarely could, the memory crystallized to perfection. His heart was at peace, the sunlight fell so gently, the pond represented tranquility itself. No doubt this memory had been formed and reformed in her mind, made more perfect than it had ever been in reality. But that fact actually told him more about who Tayn Anyinn was as a person: no one could lie in their soul itself, so this peace was truly what she sought.

He had no sein arts that could equal her polished memory, but Canumon had already planned for this. Instead of letting her overwhelm him, he responded with the rush of passions that he had prepared. She would *feel* the years of sweat in Nolese arts, the seething hatred surrounding him, the desperate drive to find a place for his family.

Canumon had thrown himself so fully into the sein of it that he took several heartbeats to recover, moments in which his opponent could easily have ended his life. Instead, as he returned to himself in the present, Canumon saw that she stood opposite him, her steel sword hanging loosely.

The sein sword had vanished along with the moment.

For a long time she simply regarded him without expression. He wanted to imagine that he could see a reflection of what he had passed to her, mingled with the tranquility of her sword, but that was self-deception. She was too old and familiar with her own soul to be so easily shifted, or at least if she had been, he would never see it on her face.

"The duel is over," she said at last, returning her sword to its sheath. "You have earned your right to a true challenge to settle in Taynol Valley. Our clans will negotiate the terms."

With that, she turned away and the mansthein beside the Lonely Diamond released sighs of relief. Canumon simply stared, wondering if he wanted what he wanted.

Anyinn

Though Anyinn wasn't sure what level of ferocity was appropriate for a young girl, she couldn't help but feel uncertain as she fended off her daughter's attacks. There was no real danger to either of them, as Heraenyas's juvenile sein made it easy to avoid any injuries. She was sure that the girl knew that, given the respect she had for her parents, and passion was better than apathy.

And yet... she didn't like how the girl threw herself into each technique. It was one thing for her daughter to possess a different quality of sein and another for a girl so young to strike with such a vicious edge. Not long ago Anyinn had smiled while facing an opponent, but the grin as her daughter caught herself on the ground and lunged forward again...

Deciding that it had gone on long enough, Anyinn used her full speed to end the sparring. It took so little effort to sweep Heraenyas off her feet with the flat of her blade and catch her in her arms, tumbling the girl end over end before depositing her on the ground.

All at once, Heraenyas was laughing like she had as a much younger child, face so utterly free of anger that Anyinn doubted if she had seen anything at all. She had been facing so many grim or bloodthirsty adults, it would be no surprise if her awareness of others had been knocked askew.

"You're doing well, daughter." Anyinn knelt down beside her, sword across her knees. "But very few warriors can safely throw themselves toward an opponent like that, and you're not one of them, not yet."

"I know, but it's so fun." Heraenyas stifled her giggle and abruptly looked too serious. "You've been so busy. And Father is always talking to boring people. You didn't even tell me what happened. Did you really fight the Deathspawn to keep them out of the valley?"

"Where did you hear that?" Though Anyinn kept her tone neutral, her daughter knew her too well, drawing back with a frown.

"You told me. You told me and Father when you were going out to fight."

"No, why did you call them Deathspawn?"

"Oh, *everybody* knows that!" Heraenyas regarded her as if astonished that her mother could be so ignorant. "The Legend says that the Dark Lord will lead all the Deathspawn to destroy the world and the Hero will lead everyone to stop him."

"Not all stories are true, Heraenyas." Anyinn set her sword aside and settled onto the tile beside her daughter. "You remember when you and your cousins told me that a flying dragon got your clothes all muddy?"

"But that... that was just being silly! It wasn't a... a Legend. Everyone is saying it, and now there are even *Deathspawn* just like in the stories..."

"I'm not sure there are. They might not be exactly the same as us, but they're alike in one way: some are good and some are bad. You shouldn't call them names and tell cruel stories about them."

The somber words made Heraenyas settle back, though it was obvious that she would require more than that to refute the powerful evidence of childhood rumors. She tucked her robes around herself and stared up thoughtfully. "But you did fight him, right? Everyone says you did."

"Yes, but it was no different than when I duel your aunts or uncles. Just a way of resolving disagreements."

"Did he have big horns and fires for eyes? I heard that they're as tall as trees and just as big around and they use huge axes bigger than me."

"The one I met was about my size, though I think some are taller. He does have small horns." Anyinn put a hand on her daughter's shoulder and rubbed it as she thought back to their encounter. Though she did remember how Canumon's eyes nearly glowed, what stuck with her was the human depth in them. "He didn't have fires for eyes. They were red, but that's not such a strange color, is it? There are people with all sorts of different colors."

Heraenyas settled back, deeply disappointed. Anyinn wasn't sure how far her words had reached, but before she could consider how to approach her daughter, she felt another presence. One so powerful that she reached for her sword before recognizing it.

Feinouya Tayn entered the small building where they had been training with a rush of sein, as if she had run the entire distance and stopped only at the entrance. The head of the entire Tayn clan had every fold of her robes immaculate and every pin in her hair precisely placed, but Anyinn saw the tension in the older woman's eyes. She had guided their clan through feuds and droughts and worse, yet now she looked more apprehensive than Anyinn had ever seen her.

"Auntie Feinouya!" Heraenyas hopped to her feet and bobbed a polite bow. Normally Feinouya might reprimand a child for addressing her so casually, even a favorite child, but today she barely gave the girl a glance.

"I need to speak to your mother, girl. Go and train."

Though disappointed by this as well, Heraenyas nodded, picked up her sword, and trudged to the door. She lingered outside the entrance, hoping to eavesdrop, but a glance from Anyinn sent her on her way. As soon as she was gone, a fist of tension closed around the room. Even though there was no urgent danger, Anyinn straightened her back and placed her hand on the hilt of her sword.

"What is it, Feinouya Tayn?" Anyinn tried to discern more from the other woman's face, wondering what could have required the head of their clan to visit personally. They had been in correspondence to arrange the rites, of course, but Anyinn had not expected any direct involvement.

"We've scheduled the challenge rite to take place thirty days from now," Feinouya said. "The terms are still being decided, but it will likely be a series of five or seven duels. Yours will be the first, at the thirty day mark, with perhaps several days in between the others."

It was a considerable delay, but that fact was obvious and Feinouya hated when people stated the obvious to her, so Anyinn shifted to the next step. "Why are you delaying the rites?"

"Because we're getting tangled deeper and deeper in this quagmire." Feinouya clasped her hands together, the fingers that had rebuilt a clan with raw force strained white. "If this was just another clan, you could defeat their champion and throw them out. I'd fight one of the duels myself. But there's an army sitting in eastern Nol and I don't think a loss would be accepted."

"Then is our goal to negotiate terms that will allow a few concessions?"

"I don't know. This is just buying time." Feinouya took a deep breath and finally faced her. "The Nolese Coalition is pretending that this isn't a challenge to Nol itself. That means that we'll be facing their best, the equivalent of many mansthein clans together. And they have masters, Anyinn. Masters who are my equal and... perhaps even worse, if the stories are true."

As the silence stretched, Anyinn realized that the head of their clan might be looking for reassurance instead of giving commands. Yet mere words would accomplish nothing, so Anyinn sought another angle of attack. "Why not accept a simple rite and allow one family to enter Taynol Valley? Even if they intended to follow with more, you could block them at every step, and potentially draw in other clans."

"It wouldn't be accepted by our allies, because they're treating this as an invasion. They want us to fight on behalf of a nation that refuses to join us in battle."

"I can fight one duel for you, but no more. My opponent... I believe that we are roughly equal and that he is not without honor. Would neutral results and further delays benefit us?"

Feinouya regarded her somberly, then suddenly let her hands fall to her sides. "Only if I can acquire allies capable of balancing those our opponents will bring to bear. And I don't know that I can. Going to any other clan would be a sign of weakness and place us in their debt. Asking a clan from Tur-Nol would be a betrayal. I can find perhaps one warrior from Estronn, but we need more."

So that was the true reason for the visit: Anyinn had traveled further beyond the lands of Nol than most of the clan. "I assume you've already spoken to our allies in the port cities and no masters from Teralanth or Reynt will answer?"

"There's no time for a sea voyage - we need someone who can run overland."

"Then you've made it clear that we have only one choice: we need to draw an ally from the Chorhan Expanse."

"Barbarians?" Feinouya regarded her skeptically even though she must have known that was the only conclusion. "I've fought a few Coran knights with some spine, but their sein is not like ours. They could never stand in one of our duels."

"But there are other groups in the Expanse. I spent some time with the Rhen tribes and met some of them with arts similar to ours." Anyinn smiled at the memories despite the circumstances. "But if the situation is truly so dire, then you need to find one of their best. The greatest of their warriors are called the Four Winds, and I have heard that the West Wind dwells on the border between Estronn and Nol."

"Even if someone could find them and return in time, would it be enough? Can you promise me their strength would be adequate?"

"No. But I trained under masters stronger than you who claimed that the Four Winds were greater than they. The West Wind in particular is said to enjoy foreign lands and strange challenges. His price might not be so high, if you can convince him of our cause."

"Then perhaps that is our only choice." Feinouya turned to her and extended a hand, which Anyinn kissed gracefully. "Thank you for your words, Anyinn. And if I have not said it... thank you for representing us so effectively. The burden that has fallen to our generation..."

She drifted off, and though propriety insisted that Anyinn should remain silent, she had too little time left for such things. "If I can offer any advice about negotiating with the Rhen, I will give it. And you know that you have my sword in the duels to come. Thirty days?"

"No, you must leave soon. Representatives from both sides will be meeting in the Straedi territory, north of the valley. One of the great lodges is being prepared and I need you to go. Avoid any violence, but learn what you can of them."

Concern about leaving her home faded into a smile as Anyinn considered what that would mean. "I think I can do that."

Canumon

After days of talk about how the humans were all brutes living in austere fortresses, the expansive lodge seemed to make no impact on the other mansthein at all. Canumon had yet to press any of them on the matter, so he could only wonder how they saw such a grand complex and changed nothing about their opinions. Perhaps they just defaulted to thinking they were back in civilization.

He, at least, couldn't spend any time in the great lodge without considering it. The name suggested a smaller building, but the mansthein and human factions were placed on opposite sides of a vast complex. Much of it was built to impress, wide marble walkways with towering pillars along the sides, but even the smaller buildings for staff were well-constructed and in good repair. That spoke to the strength of the clan that owned it more than the grand construction.

It was technically a place of peace, though he saw that it had been made with war in mind. Not for a siege of armies, but a siege of powerful warriors. The walkways were stabilized for jumping, the roofs reinforced by redundant pillars so they would not easily collapse, the angles of the windows providing defenders with a moment's initiative.

At least their personal quarters were built for their defense as far as he could tell, instead of being a prison or a death trap. Moving from place to place with no time to settle still left him disgruntled. Gowanisa seemed to adapt easily, but Laghy was fussier than usual.

His wife emerged in the kitchen while he was brewing neth, bouncing Laghy while he whined and squirmed. Canumon saw the weariness in her eyes and belatedly realized that he should have taken the boy for a time, since he soon wouldn't be able to. He didn't see any incrimination in her eyes, only exhaustion.

"Weren't you going to go meet the human?" she asked, rubbing one eye. Laghy whined and grabbed her arm as it rose, trying to pull himself higher.

"I didn't get a response, but I need to wait for the neth anyway." He gestured at the kettle, completely uselessly. "If no one comes, I'll meditate until noon and then come back to take Laghy. If the humans throw me out... I'll be back a lot sooner."

"They won't throw you out. Not with the army itching for a fight." Gowanisa started to work at something on the stove, but sniffed the tea with a look of distaste and shuffled away. He gave her a kiss on the cheek and let Laghy bite his finger for a while, though when she was this tired, she just grunted in response.

Once the neth was fully brewed, Canumon picked up the kettle and two porcelain cups. This had been a risk from the beginning, so he was only a little nervous to leave their quarters. Perhaps the day would be simple meditation and a failure on every other level, but he wasn't willing to wait for that long and endure the maneuvering of so many politicians.

As he left the mansthein-controlled side of the lodge, he reflected that his wife was right: this was a military position that wouldn't be idly challenged. Towd Catai stood guard, looming masses of muscle that always intimidated humans. He felt small and shabby next to them, even if he probably could have taken any of them in a fight. Being so bulky would have made it impossible to perform most of his techniques... though he wouldn't have refused their iron skin. They probably didn't have neck pain when they got up in the morning, either.

Entering neutral territory, Canumon looked back once and considered the crimson eyes at the other side of the walkway. All at once, the human fear became much clearer to him. Even for those who saw beyond the foreignness, the mansthein represented an existential threat to the balance of clans.

With luck, there was one human who wasn't afraid. Assuming the message had even reached her.

A pagoda sat at the end of a walkway between the two branches of the complex, mostly unused. Canumon sat down and poured a cup of neth for himself while he waited. It wasn't his best kettle, but it carried his sein clearly and didn't taste of fear or anger. That would be enough, if it mattered at all.

For a time he stared out into the mists covering the mossy crags beneath the clan lodge, then he shifted into his meditation. He was just about to consider the day a loss when she settled down on the opposite bench.

"Good morning," Anyinn said. "There was considerable discussion about whether or not your invitation was a trap."

"You told your superiors?" Canumon asked, but was gratified when she shook her head.

"Only my husband. I'm a swordswoman, so I'll try a direct thrust: does this meeting compromise our position in some way I'm not seeing?"

"I just wanted to talk. Cup of neth?"

She regarded him for a time, then nodded. They sat too far apart to make that easy, and he wondered if her back ached like his did. To his surprise, she drew her sword and adroitly flicked the unused cup into the air, catching it on the flat of the blade. Canumon filled the cup and she slid it back to her other hand for a sip.

They drank in silence for a time before she nodded. "This is good, but I suppose I should not be surprised. You've been brewing this since you came to Nol, no doubt."

"We have neth back on Orphos, too." Canumon let a bit of sein flow through the kettle, reheating it, then refilled his cup. "There are even places like this there, though they aren't controlled by clans. We have more in common than our superiors want to admit."

"That's true." Anyinn took a slow sip, eyeing him over the rim of her cup. "But not everything is so simple. They don't grow humans as large as those huge fellows you have guarding your side."

"Those are the Catai, specifically Towd Catai. They weren't born that way, as I'm sure their mothers were grateful. But instead of undergoing a natural rebirth, they go through a very expensive artificial one. It leaves them tough and strong, though-"

"Rebirth?"

And like that, the distance between them seemed just a little further. Canumon was no fool, to think that humans had the same life cycle as mansthein, yet he'd still neglected to consider the difference. He withdrew his mind for a time, trying to consider everything from outside himself. No doubt this conversation had occurred before, but not for the two of them.

"I've seen how adolescent humans go through an uncomfortable period of time in which they mature," Canumon said carefully. "For us, that period is faster but much more uncomfortable. In the distant past, it was different, but today the process can be hastened, and so it is called a rebirth. As that technology has improved, we've gained the ability to create warriors far larger than other mansthein."

"You give adolescents that much power?" Anyinn's eyes drifted toward the mansthein position and he could see her thoughts darting in different directions, like fish in a pool. Hopefully he could catch them in time.

"That would be a terrible idea. No, most of them became Catai on their second rebirth, or even third. One rebirth is necessary for maturity and is considered a birthright, though of course some are better than others. Beyond that, rebirths are earned. Only warriors who have proved themselves competent and suited to the process can become Catai."

"I cannot say that the idea of going through adolescence repeatedly appeals to me." The human woman took a sip and in that short time seemed to reconsider. "Though I suppose I did change again, when I passed beyond my ability to bear children. Perhaps it's not so different."

Though Canumon could have said a great deal on that subject, he hesitated. In some way, it felt like the subject was not his to share, though he questioned that judgment. In Laenan culture, it would be no concern at all for men and women to discuss such things, but it was anathema to Feinan mansthein. Despite having lived in Nol for so long, he wasn't completely certain how humans approached such questions.

After giving him some time to answer, Anyinn shrugged and continued. "You implied that it happens repeatedly, or at least it can. That seems... wasteful, in a sense. Are you not adults after your first rebirth?"

"We become adults after one," Canumon agreed, "but further maturation is necessary in some cases. You may not have seen them, but some mansthein have natural armor that needs to be regrown as they age. Others lose teeth or claws throughout their lives, and only rebirth can restore them."

"That isn't so different. But there really are many types of you, aren't there? I've traveled far and met many different sorts of humans, but in comparison..."

Canumon considered his response cautiously, wondering whether it was treason. Speaking of divisions within the mansthein empire was unpatriotic at best and potentially revealing weaknesses to their enemies. But Anyinn, seated across from him and calmly drinking his neth, was no enemy. So Canumon took a deep breath and decided to explain further.

"To tell you of all the mansthein would be a long lecture, and I think you might be tired of lectures after so many years." He raised an eyebrow at her and got a slight smile in response. "But there are several groups you can tell apart at a glance, though even those have different peoples and cultures. I'm Laenan mansthein, and you can usually tell us by our hair, horns, and almost human-like ears. My wife is Feinan, of the type you've seen elsewhere: no hair on the head and bone ridges to defend the ears."

"You're married?"

"With one child. And you?"

"Married with three." She seemed about to speak again, then suddenly paused and instead took a thoughtful sip from her cup, the last drops rasping.

In the silence, Canumon rose to refill her cup and his own as well. As comfortable as the conversation had been, it all abruptly felt too personal and direct. He did want to know her better, but they met between war camps and faced a potential duel to the death.

To know one another might feel warm and personal, but it wasn't enough. Like single rocks thrown over a chasm instead of a bridge.

"It isn't fair of you to answer so many questions," Anyinn said abruptly. "I think you already know us well, but do you have any questions? Not regarding military matters, of course."

"Of course." He considered for a moment, only to realize that he had few questions appropriate for the moment. "When humans talk about myths and legends, sometimes they speak about a *singular* legend. That is where the name 'Deathspawn' comes from, I think. Can you tell it to me?"

She blinked and bought time with another sip, then slowly shook her head. "That is... just a tale. A popular one, told all over Nol and even beyond, but just a story. The whole recitation takes some time, but in essence... the world is threatened by inhuman monsters who wish to consume everything. A hero, the greatest of all heroes, steps forward and goes on an adventure like any wandering warrior. He defeats the Deathspawn champions and the Dark Lord who commands them, eradicates them all, then peace is restored."

Panic stabbed deep into Canumon's heart like a lance. He didn't know how he managed to suppress the worst of it, suddenly reeling. To have it all laid out so clearly was bad enough, and to refer to a Dark Lord.. "That is... a terrible story."

"I was never fond of it." Anyinn must have seen some flicker of his reaction, because she sat back somberly. "But that type of story needs enemies to triumph over. Are you telling me that the mansthein have no such stories?"

"None in which peace is restored by committing genocide against an entire people! We've gone to war amongst ourselves many times, but the goal was always to draw in the defeated people and strengthen one another. I... do not recommend that you tell that story to any other mansthein."

"Is a story of empire any better? Our story suggests that there will be a terrible threat that requires violence, then that time will pass and there can be peace. But an empire only offers peace at the end of a sword. It cannot end until it has dominated everyone, and perhaps not even then."

"I'm not part of the empire. Not any longer." Canumon set his cup down sharply and fixed his eyes on hers, not flinching from the human darkness. "But you can't mistake the Feinan vision of empire for the mansthein vision. Some merely want allies and trading partners. The Laenan vision of expansion has never been conquering, but proving that our ways are better, that they have something to offer everyone."

"I mistrust that confidence more than a simple expanding empire. A warrior who believes he is stronger can be proven wrong, but a warrior who believes she is righteous will fight until the bitter end. I have seen too many clans believe their martial arts or their culture are so superior that they need to be spread to everyone else. A cruel oppressor might relent, but a righteous oppressor will continue doing what they believe is right no matter the consequences."

"That may be so, but I would take misguided ideals over tales of victory through the complete extermination of the enemy." True thought it was, he couldn't help but think how quickly those lofty ideals had turned on him when he married Gowanisa.

Throughout the entire conversation, their voices had rarely risen, yet the tension boiled underneath like the neth in the kettle. Canumon realized that this was exactly what he should have expected. The two of them were not cocky young warriors, to squabble and start impetuous fights. But such fights were soon broken, whereas when two veterans soberly decided to go to battle...

"You know, it's funny." Canumon leaned back against the railing behind him and gazed out over the valley, the sunlight beginning to burn away the morning mists. "You can offer someone a gift you believe is the most beautiful thing in the world, only to find them repulsed by it. I think Laenan ideals have something to offer, but you're right, not everyone agrees. Including many mansthein."

"I may... also have spoken too quickly." Anyinn gave him a human smile that was difficult to read. "Empire and dominance are common to all people. Yours may have sharper teeth, but it's the same technique by a different name. You shouldn't be mistaken for inhuman monsters."

"There's that word again." She had been offering peace, and he didn't want to squabble, but Canumon couldn't bring himself to stand down. "The way you say 'inhuman' has always troubled me."

Anyinn blinked and then shook her head. "Consider it a trick of language. I wouldn't be offended if you had such a word as 'inmansthein'. In fact, I would consider it an honor if your people come to see the 'manstheinity' of humans."

"It isn't the same. I've heard this in several languages and I don't think humans understand how arrogant it sounds. You believe that the greatest compliment that can be paid is to be *like you*. Naming your own ideals after yourself is... astonishingly self-absorbed."

"The word might seem arrogant applied to your people, but what can we be except ourselves? I stand by the word: it might not always represent our actions, but it represents our ideals. When we speak of humanity, we speak of kindness, depth of emotion, everything that we aspire to."

"And you name that concept after yourself." Canumon sat forward, caution forgotten as he raised a claw in her direction. "No mansthein would ever say that. Our words are different, and I can't even translate the concept into Nolese."

"Try."

"In Futhik we do have a word like 'manstheinity' but the meaning is different. It refers to mundane facts like our physical natures, or the essence we all have in common. But we have a completely different word that represents our ideals. This is no trivial point: humans seem to believe that their ideals dwell inside them, that to be truly human is to be laudable. Even the most grandiose of mansthein poets would never glorify our fundamental natures like that."

Suddenly he realized how passionately he had been speaking, and how recklessly. In the beginning, he had planned this meeting to allow the two of them to know one another outside combat, to form a bridge between them. He had expected argument, yet now he found himself condemning her entire species.

Anyinn let out a low laugh. "Perhaps it would be easier for us to just fight, no?"

"Maybe so." Canumon realized he was grinning and pulled back. He might have failed, but in this he wasn't fighting alone. The human woman drank the rest of her cup in a single swallow and approached him to pick up the kettle.

"You brew neth well, but let me show you how it's done."

Anyinn

They claimed that it was a test of strength, but the truth was that Anyinn was simply restless. All around the Straedi lodge, armed warriors grimly watched the other side or jostled for superior position. She and Canumon were forced to be the linchpins of it all, representing far more than themselves and yet forced to wait as their superiors attempted to prepare.

In contrast to that omnipresent pressure, dueling was deeply relaxing.

Without any intent to harm one another or need to win, they were free to exhibit everything they could do. She found Canumon to be a polished and creative warrior, sending her mind wandering into new considerations. With more at stake she would have forced herself to remain focused, but instead she could enjoy their fight as a work of art created between them. Especially the beautiful moment when he imitated her Tranquil Blade, which send her back to contemplate her own technique.

For the first time in days, she wrote more in her manuscript and actually felt it carried some meaning. Her sein arts might not revolutionize the world, but they did have something to offer. Yet before she could gain insight into any combat skills, she found herself writing about everything that had taken place between them, the sein of her techniques still entangled with the events that had produced them.

There was little else to do, given the restrictions placed on both of them. She could leave to visit her family on occasion, but her presence was generally required to continue the fiction of the upcoming rite. Each chance to spar with Canumon was relished, as they could only justify so many meetings in the name of preparing for the duel. Repeatedly facing him hand to hand put her in the mind of a friendly contest within the clan, though no one else seemed to share her interpretation.

It ended with a nearly ritualized finish. He advanced with his foot technique, which she'd begun to think of as Surging Leviathan. She countered with Waterfall Cascading Upward, evaded his variation on Punishing Willow, and then pierced him with the Tranquil Blade.

This time, she found herself flooded with memories of Canumon and his wife training together, both past and present. The simple affection in his sein was strangely touching, though she still wondered if it wasn't calculated. She wished that she could show him moments of her own, but her memory of that day by the lake was effective because it was pristine and unchanging. Instead she simply tried to impart all of herself into her blows as they fought.

Her sword was no longer disabling, Canumon merely sighing in satisfaction and rolling his shoulders. "The peacefulness you can press into one moment is truly remarkable. It makes for a very relaxing end to the spar."

"I don't mind the glimpses into your life either," Anyinn said. They no longer bothered to bow to one another, simply went to sit on the bench beside the training ground. That day, Canumon sat back and stared skyward.

"Some mansthein philosophers have suggested that using memories in sein directly is a mistake. I imagine that this idea isn't unfamiliar to humans, but what do you think?"

"You say 'some philosophers'... are you putting your voice in their mouths?"

"I'm taking their words for my thoughts. I think, after all of this, that I've come to know you, at least a little. Based on what I know, I wondered if you were uncomfortable with forging your memories into weapons."

"No, not truly." Anyinn hesitated, knowing that he deserved a better answer than she had ready at a moment's notice. There were indeed human philosophers and warriors with similar opinions on sein, but it was impossible to distill her experiences with them, much less all their words, into a simple answer. "Sein is our selves, and it has never struck me as right to separate our souls from our actions."

"Does anyone?" Canumon stretched his back and eased deeper into the seat. "Most people draw off an abstraction of their total experiences, not specific memories - even you. I haven't heard of anyone trying to use sein wiped of everything they are."

"Certain Coran groups do, and it doesn't seem to be as ineffective as you might think. You'll certainly never find their warriors accidentally losing control due to the emotions they're handling, or injuring themselves with improper sein flow."

"Huh. I've never been that far north."

"But as for me..." Anyinn knew what she wanted to say by that point, it was just a question of reconsidering her words and deciding if they were worth speaking. "I fight with everything that I am, including my memories. Separating myself, as if mother and warrior are two different people... that has always struck me as an... abdication of responsibility. Those I've raised, I raised as a warrior. Those I've killed, I killed as a mother. Violence and peace contain one another."

Canumon shifted back and actually considered her words. Most warriors in Nol preferred their clearly defined roles, and from what she'd come to know of the mansthein, she didn't think they were any more receptive to the idea. But even if he didn't agree, Canumon would always listen.

They said nothing for a time, subconsciously recovering their sein flow after the battle. At a distance, she could see a few lesser members of the Tayn clan in the windows, trying to peer at them without being seen to do so. Entirely ineffective, against a fully trained warrior, but she simply ignored them. Judging from the movement of Canumon's eyes, he noticed as well and didn't dismiss them so quickly. No doubt being surrounded by staring humans was less comfortable for him.

"We might be able to find a more private location," Anyinn said, "if it bothers you."

"Let them look. I'm less intimidating than the Catai, so it might help them get used to us."

"Very understanding of you. But, you see, humans don't only tell stories of heroic genocide. Romances are always a popular subject on the stage, and the more unlikely the romance..." She let the words trail off as soon as she saw the understanding in his eyes: she was telling him nothing that he didn't already know.

"The mansthein soldiers here have made similar comments. They're young men, mostly far from women during their service. By which I mean that they are not particularly creative when it comes to personal interactions."

"No one has ever said such a thing of human men."

Canumon cracked an abrupt smile that showed just a glint of teeth before his lips closed again. Despite her uncertainty about his smile, Anyinn thought that it was authentic. They had gradually mapped out a shared sense of humor, which was remarkable in itself: in Anyinn's travels she had seen a truly baffling number of things considered funny, yet she could jest with a man from another species.

"So long as the rumors don't undermine the legitimacy of our duel," Canumon said eventually, "then I'm not bothered by it. A more private location might not help the gossip, but would *you* prefer that? We can fight however is easiest for you."

"It's no concern at all. No one who knows me could possibly think such a ridiculous thing."

"You're the very model of a perfect Nolese wife, except you fight with a sword instead of your hands. Highly scandalous."

Though she smiled, Anyinn felt a sudden impulse to say more. She wasn't certain if it was the residual sein reflecting memories of his family or simply the opportunity to relax, but the space between them yawned free and open. When she began to speak, Canumon heard the shift in tone and listened carefully.

"I do try to appear a model Tayn warrior, because it benefits me, but I'm only a woman, not the faithful wife from some tale. To be honest, I did come close, once..." She sat back and thought to that summer so many years ago. "I was assigned to train a man several years younger than me from an allied clan. He was desperately in love with me, and the attention was flattering. I never truly considered it, but I was just starting to grow old and his adoration was so warm... but it couldn't be. You may not teach students, but I think you understand."

"A responsibility not to be violated. What happened?"

"I realized that I had gone too far, even if only emotionally. I sent him to another instructor with my commendation and apologized to my husband." That part of the memory lurked starkly free of any nostalgia. "Noreinu had noticed and even wondered. When I saw what that small uncertainty did to our relationship, I vowed to guard myself more closely in the future."

"Very noble of you."

His brief response caught her attention and Anyinn regarded him carefully. Though some aspects of mansthein body language were different, the slight shift in his posture represented unmistakable discomfort. "Have I said too much? Implied judgment? I meant no offense."

"None taken." Canumon was silent for so long that she thought he might intend to cut off the conversation there. "I wasn't as faithful as you were. It was only once, but..."

"You needn't speak about it i-"

"She was a brilliant fighter who was with our company for a short time. We intersected only in the brief period of time that it took her to surpass me. The women who escape some parts of Orphos... no, it doesn't really matter. I let passion get the better of me and didn't think about who might be hurt. Gowanisa didn't realize, and I hurt her when I came clean. I still think about that at times."

Anyinn remained silent, giving him space to say more, but he sat lost in the memories. She wanted to affirm him in some way, but the differences between them lay too stark. Eventually she asked her true question: "And yet you remained together with her. The last thing I want to do is judge you, but I think that would be difficult."

"It was. But we chose each other before, so we decided to choose each other despite it." Canumon shook his heard, returning to the present day. "I think Gowanisa dealt with it by blaming the other woman. It's true that she pursued me, but not relevant. I cared more about what seemed right in the moment than what mattered most. Since then, I've been more suspicious of my heart."

"That's probably wise."

"I try not to think about it. Not because it's uncomfortable, but because every time I remember it, I worry that I change the story just a little more, rubbing off the sharp edges. That's the bitter thing about memories."

"Especially memories forged into blades?" Anyinn regarded him with a smile that she hoped didn't dismiss the weight of what he'd said. "Is that what this was all about in the end?"

"No, it wasn't intentional." Suddenly he was giving that relaxed smile again. "On a technical level, you made a good choice with your Tranquil Blade. On a personal level, I believe that you understand exactly what you're doing. I just always hesitate when it comes to these things, because it all seems so messy to me."

"You've given me something to think about. I've told many of my students that their hearts will lead them true, if they avoid poisoning them. But perhaps anything that is healthy in its place becomes poison in excess or at the wrong time."

"Or poison is something we define for ourselves."

They remained silent for a long time after that, not thinking about how their time together dwindled away. Though they could justify time spent resting following their practice duel, eventually it would become suspect. Even if everyone watching in the windows could see that they were simply talking, they were embroiled in politics much worse than matters of the heart.

Yet Anyinn wasn't ready for their conversation to be over, not yet. She realized that as well as they knew one another in combat, they sparred only with polished techniques and polished words. As much as she had said about her husband and children, she'd shown only a few of their many facets. All at once, Anyinn was no longer satisfied by that.

"Canumon, can your wife and son travel?"

He shot a glance at her, sensing the change. "They came with me by choice and the military won't hold us here. But what do you really mean?"

"I wish to extend an invitation from my family to yours. Bring both of them and come to our home. My sons have moved far away, but you could meet my husband and daughter. Then they could stop being abstractions that we throw back and forth to one another."

"It might be possible without undue suspicion, but where? When?"

"We'll find out, won't we?"

Canumon gave her another one of those mansthein smiles. "I suppose we will."

Canumon

The human died in the middle of what had otherwise been a very pleasant morning. When Canumon first heard the shouting, he assumed that it was a squabble between Laenan and Feinan soldiers, restless during the negotiations. But shouts of "Deathspawn" couldn't be mistaken, so he'd left his quarters to locate the source.

By the time he'd arrived, the man had been cut down by the Catai, his face a crushed mess under one's over-sized war hammer. The rest of the morning had been completely consumed by panicked negotiations, thrusting him forward without any rhyme or reason to try to prevent human retaliation.

To their surprise, they were met with none whatsoever. Apparently the dead man wasn't a member of either the Tayn or Straedi clans, just a mad transient with no political connections. So the story that he had attacked unprovoked was accepted on both sides and nothing came of it other than heightened security. Canumon tracked down the Catai who had been involved and spoke to them personally, but they all gave a similar story. The only difference from the official tale was that they seemed unnerved, saying the human rushed them with something worse than madness.

Increasing tensions prevented him from sparring with Anyinn, so he was all the more glad that they had already made arrangements for their family meeting. Many of the mansthein had departed to escort new arrivals, while the human clan heads began other negotiations, leaving them relatively unoccupied. Free enough for the meeting they'd planned.

"Take him," Gowanisa said, shoving their son in his direction as she struggled with her collar one-handed. Canumon hefted Laghy in one arm, which was easy enough since he was gurgling happily at all the new sights. They'd taken him outside before, but never anywhere near this deep into human territory.

"Did you need more time?" he asked. "We're arriving early, so we could have taken it."

"The boy pulled open my damn collar." She grimaced as she got it back into place, then began smoothing down the rest of her clothes. Since she looked like she needed the ritual, Canumon continued bouncing Laghy.

She wore a fitted Laenan jacket that matched his, but with a red undershirt instead of the traditional white. In place of the combat tunic she generally preferred, she had on a pair of loose pants that imitated a skirt. He'd forgotten that she still owned those, but apparently she'd kept them in a chest ever since their last feast with Laenan officers.

For his part, he mostly wore his old military outfit. He'd considered going with his usual combat robes, but decided that they were representing themselves as mansthein. Their main concession to Nolese culture were the slanted hats they both wore, borrowed from a friend deeply concerned with the latest human fashions. Canumon suspected that they would look like imitators to most humans, but hoped Anyinn and her family would appreciate the effort.

"Is that it?" Gowanisa asked. Canumon realized that although he had been tracking his environment carefully, he'd mentally considered signs of civilization as warnings to be avoided. Their directions had been imprecise and it had been important to avoid hostile humans, after all.

"Looks like it." Canumon smiled as he observed the house ahead.

It was relatively humble, given Anyinn's position in her clan, but a solidly-built home that looked far sturdier than any of his recent houses. Peaked roofs in the Nolese style, with tiles that would make them easy to traverse on foot. Only two entrances, both reasonably fortified, and the position beside a cliff provided a degree of defense on its own.

At first the lack of boval fences puzzled him until he realized that humans would have other priorities: there was a garden area spilling down the side of one hill and a pen that contained bicorns and cockatrices. More than could be managed by several people, so they must have servants or family to help them. Anyinn had told him to expect five humans but not given details.

"What's that on top?" Gowanisa shielded her eyes from the setting sun to peer at the banner atop the house. "They put up those to give signals in the human stories, right? What does purple mean?"

"An invitation to a combat challenge. A bit of a joke, but she said that they'd mark their house that way." Though there had been little doubt in his mind, Canumon was still glad for that final confirmation. They had arrived without any trouble and could hopefully enjoy a pleasant evening.

"Then we're here. I guess I'll finally get to meet this human."

"And her family."

"I suppose." Gowanisa grunted, but she did reach over and squeeze his arm. Despite his familiarity with Anyinn, this would be a different circumstance than they'd entered before. Laghy stared at the house while clinging to the side of his head and chewing on his ear.

The house remained quiet as they approached, but as they drew closer he heard a yelp and caught a flash of dark hair near the middle of the door. Most likely Anyinn's daughter, then, hopefully announcing the guests instead of terrified for her life.

By the time Canumon and Gowanisa arrived by the threshold, they were met by the other family.

For a while, they just stared.

His eyes confirmed Anyinn's presence first, but other than wearing her formal combat robes and a peaked hat, there was nothing remarkable about her. Her daughter looked like a smaller version of her, but stayed hidden behind her parents, maintaining a suspicious glare in their direction.

Anyinn's husband wasn't quite what he expected, despite how much he'd been told. Noreinu was a slender human with the quiet soul of one who had studied sein in his youth but not afterward. His coat and pants had the look of those that were expensive for the sake of being well-used, not ostentation. He wore no hat at all, which was unusual for receiving guests.

"Welcome to our home!" Anyinn broke the silence, though for a moment it remained awkward. Some Nolese clans embraced guests and some kissed the cheek, while Canumon doubted mansthein customs were relevant. In the end, she stepped to the side and gestured to several hooks along the wall. "Please leave your hats here and enjoy our hospitality."

As they did so, she left her hat on the hook alongside them. It was perhaps a bit excessive, but the symbol was clear enough: they were being invited as true guests instead of travelers. Only as they moved did sharp teeth on his ear remind him about Laghy. When Canumon pulled his son off his shoulder, he found that the boy was staring widely between the two humans.

Just as silence rose up again, Laghy let out a delighted gurgle and began smacking his claws together. Gowanisa took the boy from his arms with a fond smile and held him close, but also closer to the humans. The nearer they got, the more Laghy gurgled happily, which prompted smiles all around.

"He seems to like everyone," Gowanisa said, not as harshly as she might have. "An old friend stopped by, a Catai missing an eye with scars all over his face... Laghy thought he was the funniest thing he'd ever seen. If I don't watch him, he'll wander off with strangers."

"He seems like a delightful boy." Noreinu stepped forward to tickle the boy's cheek and Laghy did his inept best to grab the human finger. When the human stepped closer, however, Gowanisa quickly reached to catch her son's grasping hand.

"Careful, he *will* try to grab your eyes. He's never seen ones like yours before."

As if in support of that statement, Laghy lurched forward in a desperate bid to grab Noreinu's face, but the human man only stepped back with a chuckle. "Our eldest son had a thing for noses and nearly took my brother's off his face. He could have done worse if he'd had fingers like these... though your boy just seems to want to grab." Indeed, his tiny claws only gripped the offered finger.

"Oh, like I said, he's always wonderful with strangers. It's only when he's alone or with the two of us that he starts making a nuisance of himself." Gowanisa moved inward, letting Laghy get a better look at Noreinu without being too grabby.

Since their spouses had unexpectedly begun talking, Canumon shifted to stand beside Anyinn and spoke in a lower voice. "We arrived without any trouble. Are there any complications on your end?"

"None at all, Canumon Laenan." Anyinn smiled and gestured inward. "Please, let yourself relax. Tonight should be nothing but a good meal."

So it actually seemed, despite his apprehensions. The food was apparently not quite ready, though savory smells emanated from the kitchen. After a brief look at the house, they settled together around the table. Anyinn and her husband brewed neth for them, which was unusual - it was difficult enough for two warriors to collaborate on one pot, much less a warrior and an untrained civilian. When he finally had a cup, however, it proved quite good. Perhaps marriage helped the brewing process.

Though Gowanisa wrinkled her nose at the smell, she held her tongue and accepted her cup. Before she could pretend to drink, Anyinn revealed a pair of wineskins from beneath the table and handed them across.

"I don't know what you would prefer to drink, but Canumon mentioned your feelings about neth." Anyinn nodded down at the wineskins with a smile. "I like to think we could change your mind, but if not, hopefully you can find something you'll enjoy."

"Most gracious." Gowanisa raised one of them in salute and smiled back, though the moment was ruined by Laghy lurching off her lap in an effort to grab the wineskin. Naturally, Gowanisa caught him before he could fall far, flipping him back up into her lap.

"That's the real benefit of having warriors at home," Noreinu said with a chuckle. "You never have to worry about the little ones hurting themselves, so long as you can keep an eye on them."

"That can be hard enough."

As the two of them laughed, Canumon took a sip and considered the room more carefully. His back was to a wall, not that he worried overmuch about an attack. If there was any threat, it would come from outside the door, and he sat among allies. He was far more interested in catching a glimpse of the other members of the household.

The humans' daughter hid in one of the side rooms, occasionally peering out at them, often at Laghy. Since she might notice his gaze, Canumon ignored her and instead focused on the servants. There were six seats at the table, but more tellingly, slight scratches and stains in five places. That suggested that they most frequently ate together. He wasn't sure if the servants remained in the kitchen due to the guests or out of fear, judging from the glances they cast him.

When Anyinn and Noreinu stepped into the kitchen to speak with them, the conversations seemed familial. That was enough for him. The Nolese Coalition outlawed formal slavery, but lesser members of clans were often locked into positions so miserable that they were slaves by another name. He hadn't wanted to believe anything unkind about the human couple and was glad not to.

Soon enough the food emerged, a grand platter of assorted meats that must have cost them a considerable amount along with several bowls filled with mixed fruits and vegetables. Except for the meat, it was a very Nolese meal indeed.

"We weren't sure exactly what to serve," Anyinn said as she set down the last dish. "I know you need meat, but not how it should be prepared. And I'm afraid my husband doesn't eat much meat anymore, so we need to have other options."

Noreinu patted his stomach ruefully. "I still love the taste, but the older I get, the worse it is for my digestion."

"This is fine." Gowanisa picked up one of the sausages and deftly cut off a piece to give to Laghy, who insisted on holding it and slobbering over his own hands. Since his wife looked starving, Canumon decided to elaborate on her statement while she ate.

"You don't need to worry, because whatever choices you've made, you've served us a better feast than you know." He picked up the knife beside his plate and speared a strip of what looked like bicorn meat. "The majority of mansthein eat boval meat for most meals: it's filling, but bland. Cockatrices and other animals require more care, so their meat is a rarer treat."

"We don't eat them so often either," Anyinn slid graciously into her seat, "but this is a special occasion. Heraenyas, dear, are you sure you don't want to come to the table? If you want a strong body, you need to eat strong foods."

The human girl walked out of the kitchen and sat down at her place, not making much eye contact but pretending that she had never tried to hide. They all allowed her, though Canumon noted how much she stared at Laghy. He doubted that the boy could be frightening: he was too plump and giggly to intimidate anyone. Several times he thought he caught a smile on the human girl's face.

For a time they sank into the food as if the smells and tastes could bury them. As the evening continued, they began to speak as well, though the conversation remained on topics bland as boval meat. Canumon somewhat regretted the absence of the thoughtful and wide-ranging discussions he'd often had with Anyinn, yet recognized that this was also necessary. The tension slowly drained out of Gowanisa's posture and she even laughed at a few things the humans said.

Only one disruption occurred: Laghy got his hands on another piece of meat, abruptly decided that he didn't like it, and upset an entire bowl over the floor. Gowanisa began to apologize, but Noreinu and Anyinn swooped in to take care of the mess with barely a comment. It happened so smoothly that he knew it wasn't merely hospitality: those were the techniques of a couple who'd raised several children.

Though he had brought them together, as the night grew later, Laghy became more disruptive. He had eaten a few pieces of meat but now whined and tugged at his mother's shirt, demanding to be fed. She swallowed her annoyance at first until he began grabbing at her ear ridge, as he only did when he was about to throw a tantrum.

"Do you need to feed him?" Anyinn gestured toward two of the doors beside the table. "If you want privacy, you can use the room there, or it might be cooler outside."

"Thank you." Gowanisa picked up the boy and bounced him in her arms as she headed outside, which also served to mark the end of the meal.

Canumon helped take the empty dishes to the kitchen, which seemed to make the two human servants uncomfortable, though one did mumble a thanks. He snapped up one last morsel of the cockatrice meat - however they raised them here, they tasted much better than the cockatrices in mansthein villages. When he emerged, he found that the rest of the table had been cleared, but Noreinu had lit a small fire in the hearth and moved several chairs beside it.

"None of our children were so happy, at that age." Noreinu shook his head slowly with a fond smile. "If he's anything like ours, soon enough, he'll be refusing everything. Normally I consider myself a master of determining the age of children, but... how old is he?"

"Almost a year." Seeing the glances from both humans, Canumon realized that the answer surprised them. "I think that our children grow faster than yours. When they're eight years old or so, they'll spring up if you feed them enough. But then the last years go slower than I've seen with humans. Some say that you aren't really an adult until you reach twenty years of age."

"I've heard thirty." Noreinu laughed and Canumon laughed with him. Anyinn smiled, but instead leaned forward with a curious expression as she spoke.

"And when does that aging end? For mansthein without sein training, of course."

So Canumon explained what he knew, though he was no scholar. As near as he could tell, wealth mattered more than anything else, because elderly mansthein who couldn't afford a rebirth would struggle to eat. He thought that Feinan mansthein tended to die sooner but kept that to himself, since it might be nothing but gossip.

After the conversation had gone on for some time, Gowanisa returned with Laghy. Though Canumon had expected the time alone to do her good, his wife frowned and made an odd gesture at Anyinn. Whatever was communicated between them, the two women departed through the main door and he was left with the baby.

The boy was well-fed and rambunctious, so Canumon ended up putting him on the floor. He hadn't expected it, but the human girl went to play with him, a strange fascination on her face. Laghy gurgled and grabbed for her, and only then did Canumon notice that she had tied her hair back so he couldn't grab it. Smart girl. She also carried a toy warrior carved from wood, which Laghy struggled to grip and then banged against the floor. Soon the two of them were playing on the other side of the room, in the uneven manner of children at very different ages.

"It's strange to see her like this." Noreinu sat down in the chair beside him, carrying two cups of wine. Canumon accepted one, but only held it.

"She doesn't like children?"

"She's never shown any interest in such things, but she's also never been the oldest before. It was always her brothers playing soldier with her or carrying her around the house. This might be her only chance to do the same."

"Perhaps they can play together more often." Yet as he spoke, Canumon knew that it couldn't be. He took a slow drink of his wine, barely tasting it, and spoke in a lower voice. "But probably not. I assume Anyinn told you the details, but the tensions are getting worse."

"Worse among warriors. Your merchants have had time to talk to ours." Noreinu spoke lightly, but the grim look in his eyes suggested that he fully understood. "That's always the tension here in Nol. The merchants need the clans to do business, but the in-fighting is a cost they'd rather avoid."

"I've lived here most of my life."

Noreinu shook his head. "Right, sorry. Well, it doesn't make too much difference. I think a lot of the people I've spoken to would be happy to end the rite and just trade at a distance. But could it really end that way?"

"Probably not." Canumon took another drink and tried to appreciate the wine this time. "There's more going on beyond us, but that doesn't mean the fight with your wife is irrelevant. It's the story w-"

"You don't need to tell me how stories work. Stories make sense and life doesn't, so we prefer the stories. If we can't find them, we'll make them. But nobody has a story for this yet."

"Some believe they do, with this legend."

"Right, the Legend." Noreinu's cup of wine hung in his hand, nearly ignored as the man stared into the fire. "I confess I don't like how people talk about it, these days. It reminds me of something that's already irritated me as a playwright... you've seen some of the classical Nolese plays, yes?"

Canumon nodded. "A version or two."

"Then you should know that there are different versions from different authors, even before you get to the modern reinventions. What frustrates me is when people ask me what the *real* version is, as if there's a single truth. The only truth is that they're all just stories and we don't know what really happened. I'm used to holding all those differences in my head, but others... there are some who want only one story, and it's a bloody one."

"I'm not sure it's as bad as that. You were able to accept us quickly enough, even though I tried to kill your wife."

He'd meant it as a lighthearted joke, but Noreinu was staring into the fire grimly now. At first it seemed like he hadn't heard at all, before he eventually shook his head. "We did, but we're only two families. Everyone else... I don't know if this is a story that can reach them."

There wasn't much that could be said to that. The two men sipped their wine, and they would soon begin talking again, but for a time they said nothing and watched the fire.

Anyinn

"You wanted to talk?" Anyinn followed the mansthein woman outside and was surprised how cold it had become. The lights of their home and the main lantern lit the small courtyard well enough, but they generated no warmth.

"Yes, we need to settle a few things." Gowanisa turned to her with another one of those mansthein smiles and Anyinn decided just to ask. She might have been more comfortable with Canumon, yet the question seemed more appropriate for another woman.

"I'm not sure I understand how mansthein smile. When a human smiles that way, without showing any teeth, it can mean that they're insincere."

"You want to see my teeth?"

Gowanisa's face split wider and rows of knives glittered sharply. In the light of the lanterns, her eyes glowed brighter red, her pupils thin horizontal lines, and her mouth became a vicious maw. Clearly, the mansthein woman made no effort to smile pleasantly, but the demonstration was still effective.

Despite herself, Anyinn found the word "Deathspawn" coming to mind. She had noted the differences between Gowanisa and her husband before, but now they took on a more sinister cast. Most notably, Canumon had vertical pupils, while his wife's eyes were dark horizontal bars. His ears might be unusual, but they were more human than the bone ridges on Gowanisa's head. Though he had horns, the full head of hair left them less menacing than his wife's hairless visage.

The smile closed, though it became more pleased with itself than friendly. Gowanisa turned away and stared into the darkness as she answered. "Showing your teeth is aggressive, not friendly. Of course, there are many different mansthein cultures, and individuals differ. I've met some who intentionally smile with their teeth every time, or move between the two to make others uncomfortable."

"I suppose there are always some like that." Anyinn shook her head and gave a smile of her own. "Still, I'm glad to exchange friendly smiles with you instead."

"The word you want is 'polite'." Gowanisa didn't look toward her as her voice became colder. "I've never liked your type. So self-composed, so self-confident."

All at once, Anyinn realized how deeply she had misjudged the other woman. "Gowanisa, I'm sorry if I've offended you. I hope you don't believe your husband and I-"

"You see? You always think you understand."

"It's easy to throw accusations. Tell me what you want."

"I need to know who you are." Gowanisa finally turned on her, no smile at all, her eyes burning sunsets dropping into a dark horizon. "Canumon believes in your spirit, but all I've seen is that you're good at appeasement. Fight me."

"Fight y-" Anyinn cut off as a claw swiped at her, dangerously fast. "Here and now?"

"Do it." Gowanisa shifted her stance and Anyinn realized that her skirt was actually loose pants suitable for swift movements. Her voice was a hiss that wouldn't disturb anyone inside, yet she advanced with her sein boiling up inside her.

"Are you sure you want to spar now? Given your current state..." Anyinn looked down toward the mansthein woman's stomach.

It was the wrong thing to do. Gowanisa hissed "You understand *nothing*!" and then attacked her with full force.

Relaxed as Anyinn had been, she still carried her sword. She managed to resist her first instinct and instead detached the entire sheath, using it to deflect the first swipe and then strike the other woman's arm. In its sheath her sword was slightly heavier, but that disadvantage was nothing compared to holding back to avoid direct cuts.

Though Gowanisa attacked viciously, driving her back across the courtyard, Anyinn resisted being drawn into her momentum. The mansthein woman was strong, and not unskilled, but not as dangerous as her husband. Her sein granted her more brute strength but less agility, which was exactly the wrong combination against a swordswoman like Anyinn.

She could have ended the fight then and instead prolonged it, letting the momentum drive them back and forth across the courtyard, preventing their duel from disturbing the peace within. Though Gowanisa grunted and occasionally hissed, she was otherwise utterly silent, attacking with a ferocious determination.

At last they ended up against the outer wall, Anyinn restricted in the narrow space, and her opponent lunged. Before Anyinn could strike, her sword arm was caught and pinned in place. The other claw rose swiftly and drove toward her face.

So Anyinn stepped forward, bringing her forehead sharply against Gowanisa's nose. The impact staggered her, fingers loosening as she dropped several steps back and instinctively grabbed her face.

Though Anyinn prepared for a counter-attack driven by anger, instead her opponent paused. Gowanisa rubbed her nose and stared down at the blood, then suddenly smiled. Her lips parted just enough to see a bit of her teeth, and despite the lesson, Anyinn had no idea how to interpret it.

"You're not so bad." Gowanisa wiped away the rest of the blood and bared her teeth in an expression that left no doubt. "But I want to see this sein blade of yours. Do it before I-"

Using her full speed, Anyinn drove the Tranquil Blade through her opponent's chest. She poured in more sein than usual, overwhelming Gowanisa with the memory of that peaceful day. While the other woman stood stunned, Anyinn carefully lifted her sword and put the dull end of the sheath against her throat.

When Gowanisa returned to the present, her eyes remained heavy with peace from her technique. Instead of a dark line, her pupils had widened into a large bar. She slowly realized that the sword was against her throat, smiled faintly, and then dropped to sit down in the dust of the courtyard.

After a pause, Anyinn sat down alongside her with her sword across her lap. Showing herself willing to sit in the dust might help Gowanisa accept her... though Anyinn realized that she was falling into that same trap of presuming she understood everyone around her. After confronting the other woman's sein directly, Anyinn felt a deep connection, yet she thought she understood less than before.

"That's a hell of a technique." Gowanisa slowly rubbed her sternum just where it had struck. "I guess, if anything, he was underselling you. You aren't so bad."

"Thank you." Though Anyinn was glad to hear it, that admission felt like not nearly enough. Perhaps instead she needed to probe her ignorance... "You said that I didn't understand anything. You meant that about mansthein pregnancy, or something else?"

"No, you have that part right. I don't really want to talk about it." Despite her words, Gowanisa kept talking. "It isn't the same for us, not unless you want your body to be torn apart. To have a child like Laghy... well, it requires herbs and other techniques that make it more difficult to conceive."

"Then I didn't understand, but I think I might have begun to."

"Do you? Do you really? The worst of it is that a child can quicken, but then, before it comes to term..."

Anyinn's mind flowed over the hope, the pain, and a small grave behind the house. She explained none of it and her hands remained still in her lap as she instead spoke quietly. "Between our second and third child..."

Something of her thoughts must have made it into her voice, because Gowanisa turned to her with a new expression. For a time she said nothing, then she simply nodded. All at once the mansthein woman rubbed her eyes with the back of one hand, only weariness remaining. "I'm sorry. I'm just frustrated."

"You don't need to apologize."

"The part that pisses me off is that I'm going to fall right into your trap. You're the first woman I've really talked to in a long time, since the villagers don't trust me and the women in the military move too quickly." Gowanisa shook her head at herself. "I want children, but I don't want to be just another Feinan female. I'm training, but I worry I'm stagnating my own progress."

Finally, Anyinn had returned to familiar ground. She resisted the urge to touch the other woman's arm, since she thought that would be a step too far, and instead tried to speak without any pretensions of wisdom. "I felt that all of my pregnancies made me stronger. You go through new experiences and different emotions... all of those can't help but deepen your sein. Yes, I lost progress on days when I was too sleep-deprived to train, but that experience tempered me in the end."

"Maybe for you. But as much as I love Laghy, he took a huge piece of myself. Sometimes, when it's difficult... I don't know if it was worth it. And I immediately feel guilty, but then I worry that I'm killing myself with bitterness, associating my own children with failure... dammit!" Gowanisa abruptly took a swipe at her, though a halfhearted one. "Did you manipulate my mind with that sein strike? Force me to spill all my secrets?"

"I learned how to fight mostly to become friends with people," Anyinn said. For once, she seemed to hit the right tone and Gowanisa just laughed low in her throat. They were silent for a long time, sitting in the courtyard, and then the mansthein woman levered herself back to her feet.

"I'm going to go back inside before you do anything else to me. But I hope you and Canumon can find a solution to all this."

Like that, it was over and they returned to the customary warmth of the home. Inside, she discovered Heraenyas and Laghy playing with one another and both of them smiled, in human or mansthein fashion. Their husbands sat by the fire and spoke in low voices, a conversation that seemed less personal and more dire.

Once they were all together, they shared another drink and spoke of nothing as the night wore on. Laghy cheerfully rode on Heraenyas's back and chewed on her hair, shrieking gleefully at every bounce. Though their play struck Anyinn as overly risky, the mansthein parents only watched in amusement, so she kept her silence.

Gradually the two children wore down, and to Anyinn's surprise, her daughter crawled up into her lap with Laghy in tow. The boy mumbled nonsense at her and then they both fell asleep, wrapped around each other. Anyinn hadn't held two children in her lap since their boys had been young, so she let them sleep for some time before putting them to bed.

With the children asleep, they were able to discuss more serious matters. All questions of human and mansthein were set aside as they instead spoke of life in Nol. She realized just how long it had been since they'd had an adult conversation with another couple and relished it.

Eventually they insisted that Canumon and Gowanisa stay, since it was late and the children were already in bed, and all agreed to retire. Anyinn realized that the servants had gone to sleep without finishing the cleaning and began to work at it, more to give her hands something to do than for any other reason. Despite the warmth of their conversation, sleep would not come easily that night.

Before long, her husband came to join her, taking up one of the plates. He seemed lost in thought, almost like when he was consumed by new inspiration, yet he remained close by. After considering several banal statements about the night, Anyinn decided to ask what mattered.

"You have an idea in mind, don't you?"

"Maybe I do." He looked up from the plate, which he'd barely touched, and gave her a smile that needed no work to interpret. "After talking to your mortal enemy, I've been thinking about what really drives this conflict. Both of you might have been going about it the wrong way..."

Canumon

After the evening spent with the Tayn family, returning to their temporary quarters at the lodge was undeniably disappointing. They were surrounded by mansthein in a more familiar bed, but the rooms utterly lacked the worn edges that made the human house feel like a home. Canumon wished that he could earn such a home for himself, as unlikely as it seemed.

Even Laghy seemed dissatisfied, wielding a spoon against anything in range. "Nya!" he screeched. "Nya! Nya!"

"What the hell does he want?" Gowanisa growled, running a hand over her scalp. "I managed to nurse him once, but that wasn't it. He threw solid food I gave him, so I just don't know."

"Something special he got last night?" Canumon asked, but his wife just shook her head.

It could be difficult to figure out what their son wanted, as he was better at volume and emphasis than clarity. It was obvious enough that "Ca" meant him and "Oma" was mother, along with a few other words for things he wanted. But "Nya" was new, so if it wasn't a new food...

"The girl." Canumon snapped his claws together as he realized. "Do you think that's him trying to say 'Heraenyas'? He did seem to enjoy playing with her."

"Could be." Gowanisa bent down in front of him and got his full attention. "Are you asking for Heraenyas, Laghy? Do you want to play with Heraenyas?"

"Nya, nya!" He banged his spoon into her face a few times and Gowanisa sighed as she just let it bounce off her.

"I don't know if I have the patience for this, Canumon. It was already too much trouble avoiding attention, so we can't just wander over there again."

"Let me take him for a while, at least," Canumon said. "You can rest for the day."

Unfortunately, he wasn't able to keep his promise to his wife. After less than an hour wrangling Laghy, soldiers came to their chamber and demanded he go meet with the commander. There was no question of refusing the order, so he went with them and soon found himself outside the lodge grounds.

As he walked, he realized that the Laenan camp had moved near the edge of the Taynol Valley, sitting within the same cluster of hills as the lodge. It remained within sight for those with sein training, a very short run at full speed. With their presence so undeniable, it must have been approved, but he'd heard nothing about it.

Kanavakis straightened up when he arrived, pushed aside papers that looked troublingly like plans for war. "Nin Canumon. You've been with the humans more than most. Do you have any idea what they're scheming with all this?"

"I beg your pardon, Kaen?"

"I suppose these are our wages for keeping you in the dark." Kanavakis turned on him with a sour glance. "In all this time you've spent befriending the human warrior, I hope you've come to know them. Has something seemed different lately? Any sign that the human clans have changed their strategy?"

"None at all, Kaen." The answer came automatically and honestly, since Anyinn had seemed no different. As soon as he said it, he began to reconsider, wondering if their apparent friendship could possibly be a part of some subtle scheme...

"Well, you might get a chance now. They've demanded to meet with you, saying that the previous terms of the rites are unacceptable. No matter what they say, we need you to stall. Did they know about our plans? The timing is too suspicious..."

"Laenan Kanavakis, I need more information than that." Canumon put a hand on top of the commander's papers, grasping his attention in more ways than one. "First, what do you know about the differences in their strategy? Second, what is the army doing that makes the timing suspicious?"

"I don't know nearly enough about whatever the humans are scheming. Bring back whatever information you can. But as for our side..." Kanavakis looked away toward the mansthein position far to the east. "Our Zeitai - the Laenan Zeitai, I mean - had no interest in this minor conflict until a recent report apparently caught his attention. He's supposed to arrive any day now, and once he does, the balance of power will shift in our favor."

Though he had more questions, Canumon swallowed them as he thought over the import of that. He'd never come close to meeting one of the Zeitai: in his life they were reverential statues or idols. Foundations for oaths or great powers to silently beg for grace. For one of them to actually arrive...

"Your role in this is almost over." Kanavakis clapped him on the shoulder and smiled aggressively. "Just sniff out anything they're planning and hold on a little longer. Depending on what the Zeitai orders, we might not need a pretext any longer."

That was an ominous end to the conversation, but Canumon was too taken aback to argue any further. He went along with the soldiers quietly, considering how much to say. Though he did try to consider if Anyinn might be manipulating him, in the end he refused to believe it. If what their families had shared was false, he didn't want to believe in anything.

Soon enough they escorted him to an empty hill within sight of both the human lodge and the mansthein camp. This was obviously not going to be a family meeting or a relaxed spar, not with human forces already in evidence and Canumon carrying an army with him.

Yet Anyinn awaited atop the hill, and he didn't see anything false in that human smile.

When he climbed to stand opposite her, she greeted him, then lowered her voice. "Did your side bring anyone to eavesdrop?"

"I think they're ordinary soldiers." He resisted the urge to look over his shoulder at his escort, trusting his sein senses to have taken their measure. "Have things changed on your side?"

"Yes, but there's no reason to fear. We have a new plan." Anyinn's face abruptly became serious beyond belief, an expression wholly different from the quiet focus he remembered in combat. "If we're interrupted, I'm telling you that clan elders have met and decided that the initial challenge rite was never properly accepted. New terms must be negotiated."

"And this plan is nothing to fear?"

"Yes, because my husband had a moment of brilliance. He claims that he was inspired by your conversation, so perhaps you already suspect. The core problem that stops all of us is that both sides *must* win the challenge. A human loss would lead to backlash, and a mansthein loss could lead to war. A tie could be worse than either. I believe the two of us know one another well enough that we could fake any result and make it believable, but there are no results that lead to what we want."

Canumon folded his arms, trying to make it look like posturing. "We could make any result plausible, but I don't know about believable. People often don't believe what's directly in front of them, if it isn't what they want to believe."

Anyinn accepted his point with undiminished optimism. "That won't matter, if we position ourselves properly. The secret is not to negotiate any compromise, but to find a way for both sides to believe they've won. That isn't as impossible as it sounds, because we don't want exactly the same things."

"I'm listening. How does rejecting our challenge help with that?"

"Because it's a vicious and underhanded move on our part." A shadow of a smile almost made it onto her face before she continued. "The new terms will appear to be beneficial to you, but they will in fact be a trap. Even if you win, you'll receive marginal land considered unimportant by the Coalition. Any clan that took such a deal would be humiliated, but I don't think it really matters to your leaders."

"Huh. Interesting." Canumon couldn't maintain the pose and slipped his hands into his sleeves to consider. "I can see how that would allow your clan to accept a loss, but I'm not so sure we'll be happy about it."

"That's why I wanted to speak with you first. You don't need farmland or political power, right? If I understood you right, what the army wants is legitimacy and a place in Nolese culture. So 'defeating' you in the game will give our clan a victory while implicitly accepting you as a legitimate participant worth defeating. But if you need better terms, they won't be fully set until both sides have argued over it."

"I'll admit it's an elegant maneuver, but that isn't what I meant."

Amusement had been lurking beneath the surface of Anyinn's expression like a fish just under the surface, but now it darted away. "What do you mean?"

"We might be able to make the merchants and the army happy, but they've brought someone stronger. Have I ever told you about the Zeitai? I... cannot understate how important they are in our society. Apparently this matter has grown so serious that one of them will be arriving. I don't know what he wants, but his presence could throw out every other plan."

"The truth is, we've been searching for masters to tip the balance as well." Anyinn considered the matter, then gave a small shrug. "But they haven't arrived yet, so we can still lay the groundwork they'll find. You don't think the plan is fundamentally flawed, do you?"

"We can still try." Canumon took a deep breath and gave her a nod that meant more than any smile. "Stick to the spirit of your husband's plan, but avoid setting terms. I'll learn what the Zeitai wants here, if I can. Then perhaps we can find terms that let both sides think they've defeated the other."

"I'll do what I can. I suspect that this Zeitai doesn't care about farmland, does he?"

"No. No, that seems unlikely." He wished that he could say more, but the new variable had thrown everything into uncertainty.

For a time they just stood and looked at each other. Two nights past, Canumon had been comfortable in a human bed alongside his wife and their peoples coming together had seemed possible. Now, on the hill with armed warriors behind them, the fact that they couldn't bridge that gap with simple understanding was as plain as the sun burning overhead.

If it was only the two of them, it would have already been over. But they were just actors in the play, and they needed to play their roles. Accepting it, Canumon gave a respectful bow from one warrior to another. Anyinn returned it and departed with a hand on her sword, never looking back.

For his part, he rejoined the mansthein soldiers and returned to the camp. Though he carefully thought through what he would say, he found that Kanavakis and most of his command tent were gone. Everything was in disarray, but he pushed through the rumors and found what he'd feared was the truth.

Zeitai Terza had arrived.

With no one to order him otherwise, Canumon left the main camp in the direction the others said the commander had departed. Soon enough, he spotted a grand pavilion in Laenan emerald. The flags that flapped at the corners were the pure Laenan crest, not crossed with the symbol of any legion or faction. Even though he'd never seen them himself, Canumon knew that only the Zeitai flew such flags.

Before Canumon could approach, Kanavakis and several of his aides intercepted him. Some of them still appeared stunned after the meeting and Canumon couldn't be sure if it was awe, fear, or simply the shock of being in the presence of a master. In any case, it was obvious from their expression that for them, nothing would be the same.

"You met with the humans, yes?" Kanavakis spotted him and brushed the matter aside. "Did you stall them?"

"Yes. They need... more time to argue about new terms."

"Time is exactly what the Zeitai wants. He's brought more people than I expected: his own elites, Voidwalkers, and I don't know who else. He wants us to avoid excess human attention while he searches for something."

"For what?"

"Hell if I know." Kanavakis lowered his voice and stepped much closer. "The Zeitai isn't alone, Canumon. He's barely spent any time in his pavilion, except to meet with local Laenans. Most of the time, he's been consulting with someone in the tent beyond."

Canumon jerked his head to the side, troubled that he had completely misread an aspect of the landscape. Now he immediately saw what he had overlooked: beyond the other camps, a pitch black tent sat atop one of the higher peaks like a predator. It was small, almost humble compared to the Zeitai's tent, yet just the sight of it filled him with a deep sense of foreboding.

"Who..." Canumon paused to clear his throat. "Who is that?"

"I don't know." Kanavakis laughed, showing all his teeth, and pulled him back toward the army. "I really don't know."

Anyinn

Even though the lodge was owned by the Straedi clan, their claim to it had been shaken. The mansthein army remained at a distance and showed no signs of advancing, and their numbers were only equal to the mustering clan branches. Yet it didn't matter: the arrival of the mansthein champion and whatever he brought with him cast an oppressive shadow over the entire valley.

Anyinn always wore her sword, but now she found herself frequently resting her hand on its hilt. Even the least trained of mansthein soldiers, who were no real threat to her, seemed filled with dark inspiration by the arrival of their leader. She had yet to even see the rumored Zeitai, but his presence dominated all the rest. Though the rite was technically their reason for gathering, she increasingly wondered if anyone would survive long enough to fight it.

Stopping on one of the walkways between two parts of the complex, Anyinn stared out through the mists. They camped beyond the eyesight of the untrained, but she could see the mansthein moving between their tents. The change in them was more than just morale, or so her heart insisted: the spirit of the valley itself was under assault.

She turned away, intending to return to her room, only to spot something shifting in the growing human camp on the opposite side of the lodge. For a moment she thought that it was an advancing army, then she realized that a new group had arrived.

Leaping off the side of the walkway, Anyinn swept her way to the group, running her eyes over them. There was a contingent of warriors from allied clans, which didn't surprise her, but there were others with little or no sein training. Aside from the group of noncombatants, she was shocked to see mere students, including some from her own school. Boulanu walked along with them, his challenge against her apparently not having disqualified him.

Before she could reach them, Feinouya emerged from the group, also moving at speed. She took an intercept course and they both came to a halt atop a small knoll as if it had been a planned meeting instead of a blockade. The Tayn clan head gave her a grim nod as soon as they stopped running.

"You've done well to take us this far, Anyinn, but time is running out. The mansthein may not respect our rules for much longer."

"Then why are you bringing defenseless students?" Anyinn kept her tone civil, but Feinouya saw the naked insubordination in the words and fixed her with a stare.

"Defenseless by our standards, perhaps, but not in a pitched battle." Feinouya tipped her peaked hat in the direction of the mansthein army. "They have three times our numbers, but most of them have received limited training. Even our students are worth several of them, so they can balance the soldiers and prevent their warriors from striking ours."

Anyinn took a deep breath, considering if she might be wrong. It was true that in times of war, when the diplomacy of challenges failed, everyone who had taken clan oaths was required to fight.

She couldn't blame Feinouya for being concerned, since the path to a peaceful resolution seemed unclear, and yet...

"You're sure it will come to pitched battle, then." Not quite a question, not quite a statement, but all she could offer if the clan head's mind had been determined.

"Not necessarily. This Zeitai could press their advantage if he wanted, but so far he seems more interested in an unknown goal. I sent word to our northern scouts to hurry, but I don't know if they'll arrive in time. We need to be prepared in case he decides to move against us."

"Are you going to meet with him?" Anyinn asked. "I dislike how they understand our objectives, but we lack information about theirs. If their goal was eradicating us, they're taking a strange approach, so I worry that we're being distracted from their true goal."

Her arguments did seem to reach Feinouya, who stared out toward the mansthein camp again. Before she could speak, they were interrupted by someone clambering up the knoll toward them. The clan head shot the man a glance that would have sent most quailing... and yet he continued to approach.

When Anyinn looked at the stranger, truly looked, the little rise of earth became a cliff. Her first instinct was that they stood in the presence of a true master, yet she had seen many charlatans in her time, and her second look revealed the man to be a warrior of middling strength. And yet when she stared at him, she felt that she stood in the presence of greatness.

It was certainly nothing about his clothes, which were patched and torn, or his hat, which was just the circle of wicker used by farmers. She didn't recognize him from their clan or as a noteworthy warrior from any nearby. Yet he carried himself as if he was the ancient Emperor of Nol, as if the fact that they hadn't bowed to him yet was insulting beyond belief.

"It is good that you have gathered our army," he said, his voice resonant, "but that is only the beginning. The Deathspawn seek to crush the hope of humanity before it can blossom, so we must strike first. If we act together, we can destroy them before they raze our lands."

"You have no right to speak to me that way!" Feinouya lunged out with a palm blow intended to disable and the stranger somehow stepped aside.

Anyinn wiped her eyes with one hand, struggling to gather her shattered impressions into true discernment. In terms of sein and raw speed, the stranger was inferior to either of them, and if he dodged one palm, he surely couldn't dodge another. Yet he evaded so easily, as if it was a trifle, that she again found herself doubting him. It was as if he simply ignored all the combat instincts she'd developed over decades and declared his presence to be all that mattered.

"Who are you?" Feinouya demanded. The man gave a bow that had no relation at all to humility.

"I am the Hero, and I have come to save humanity from the Deathspawn. You have done well to defend us for this long, but now it is time for the Legend to begin."

"Are you mad?" Feinouya looked as though she wanted to begin another technique but had forgotten everything she had learned in a surge of anger. Anyinn quickly stepped up beside her, feeling that striking him would never be the answer. If this was truly a madman, that would be cruel, but she suspected that something worse was occurring, a spiritual revolution that could not be struck down by force.

"You don't see the truth now, but you will." When he shook his head in disappointment, Anyinn felt a tug of shame. She hardened her heart against manipulations, yet there was no outside sein attempting to twist her emotions. "I tell you, the Hero has come and you will either stand with me or against me."

"If you bring the truth," Anyinn said carefully, "then show it to us. You say that you are a hero out of an old story... give us proof."

"Then I will." The man drew himself up and Anyinn realized that she was holding her breath. "Watch as I slay the first of the Zeitai. They will send more, because the one they serve is the true enemy, but that victory will be your proof. When I return, you will give me control of the clan."

With that he turned away, racing over the hills as if he intended to attack the Deathspawn camp then and there. Anyinn blinked in surprise and Feinouya stared at him before rubbing her head. "That fool... is he really?"

It seemed so, as he swept past the outer guards without hesitation. The sheer audacity of it let him penetrate their lines, all the mansthein shocked by the arrogant human who simply ran into their camp. Untrained soldiers couldn't stop him, but a sein-trained warrior finally moved to intercept, grabbing his shoulder to force him to halt.

A blow to the throat sent the Deathspawn to the ground, clutching his windpipe. Though she watched from a great distance, Anyinn thought the injury might be potentially lethal and instantly felt a surge of conflicting emotions. There was no time for any of them, because the Hero had already reached the great emerald tent of the Zeitai.

Her sight had always been better than her hearing, so she could only guess that the Hero was shouting his challenge. Several others followed him, keeping their distance when he glared at any who came close.

Finally the Zeitai himself emerged, flanked by four Deathspawn wearing identical coats. He walked with the supreme confidence of a master and should have seized her full attention, yet Anyinn found herself fixing on the coats. The buttons and elegant tails were so similar to those that Canumon and his wife had worn when visiting their house, they must be traditional Laenan garb.

Anyinn took a step back as if she could evade the realization. All at once she wasn't staring at a horde of monstrous Deathspawn, but a camp of uncertain soldiers in an alien land. Her own thoughts had betrayed her and she struggled to find the thread that had taken her to that point... and there was no time to think. A point of a light and a point of darkness seared next to one another and she heard Feinouya gasp.

Yet it was no true battle, and it couldn't be, given the vast difference between them. The madman didn't even reach the Zeitai, cut down by the four guards as soon as he approached.

Though the Zeitai still loomed ominously in her vision, she forced herself to see that he was just a man: a short Laenan man wearing elaborate robes. She encouraged herself to fixate on the details: strange loops of silver spanned the front of his coat and sleeves, too finely wrought to serve any defensive purpose, so they must be ornamental. He cast a scornful glance at the corpse of the madman, called out a few commands, and then returned to his tent.

"What kind of fool was that?" Feinouya's voice came ragged and when Anyinn turned to look at her, she took another step away. The clan head stared with bloodshot eyes, and as much as Anyinn wanted to ask her about what they had witnessed, she couldn't bring herself to speak.

The mansthein didn't retaliate for the attack, yet the result could never be called peace. Everywhere she went in the Straedi lodge, Anyinn heard whispers of what had happened. Many of the observers seemed to have misunderstood, yet the more she heard, the more she doubted her own memories. Eventually she fled to her chambers and began writing furiously.

Even though it had nothing to do with her manuscript, Anyinn found herself grasping whatever paper she could find and recounting the events. She did it more than once, desperately, as if writing down the experience would make the inexplicable clear.

Over the next several days, the two sides remained in an uneasy stalemate. Though she had scheduled a meeting with Canumon, when she approached the mansthein side of the lodge, she was immediately met by hostile soldiers. Since the truce sat balanced on the edge of a blade, she retreated to her writing.

When she looked over her accounts, she was surprised to see that they shifted from one day to the next. Her memory of the event seemed extraordinarily clear, seared into her memory, yet she had been equally confident when she had written the earlier accounts. It troubled her to find that she had written "Deathspawn" at times when she'd meant to write "mansthein".

The worst of it all was that she felt no attack and sensed no violation of her mind. Instead the events simply mellowed like a fond memory, all pleasant sweetness and retroactive warmth.

She desperately wanted her husband, but Noreinu had yet to arrive, and in her calmer moments she thought that it was safer for him to remain away. Speaking with Canumon could also have helped her sort through the uncertainty, but the sides remained hostile. Instead the uncertainty simply stretched on and on until one day the clan head arrived in her chambers to announce the news.

The scouts had returned successful: the West Wind had arrived to fight for them.

Canumon

As much as he wanted to stay in bed, Canumon knew that the day wouldn't wait for him. With the afterglow fading, he couldn't help but think about the delicate balance with the gathering human army. Every day, the humans seemed to grow bloodthirstier, and the talk in camp was starting to consider striking first.

When Canumon swiveled his legs off the side of the bed, however, Gowanisa grabbed his arm and pinned him back down.

It was actually a traditional Feinan wrestling technique, though ending with her sprawling on top of his chest was not the traditional conclusion. His wife gripped his hair and pulled him into another kiss.

"Do you need to go?" Her teeth bit at his lip, but in the end he had to pull away.

"The humans apparently have their champion, so the rite might be superseded. Unless w-"

"I know." Gowanisa dropped against him, now demanding only a place to rest. "It's just that, for a little while, I was able to forget about all of it. As soon as we get dressed and go back out, we'll be choking on that shadow again..."

"Shadow is a good way of putting it." Canumon reluctantly pulled himself upright again and bent down to retrieve his pants. "But I'm not sure who's casting it. If things are bad for us... the soldiers are on edge, and I don't like where it's going."

"Ugh, don't remind me. Are you *sure* we can't st-"

At that moment they were both interrupted by an exuberant voice screeching, "Ca! Oma! Oma! Ca! Oma!"

Gowanisa groaned and pulled one of the cushions over her head. As soon as he had his pants tied, Canumon headed over to the room just beside theirs. It was a relief that the boy had slept so long, but now nothing would stop him from making an absolute nuisance of himself until he was given attention.

Fortunately, nothing was wrong with Laghy except his lack of anyone waiting on him the moment he woke up. Canumon let him chew on a finger and bounced him around for a while, which was enough to make him happy again. That made him the only person in the entire Taynol Valley in a good mood, or so it seemed.

Eventually their son insisted on seeing his mother as well, so Canumon carried him back to the bed. He smiled fondly at how

Gowanisa had wrapped herself in the sheet, but as he sat down, his lower back twinged. All at once, he looked down at the two of them and realized that they'd grown old. Their training might have kept them in excellent physical condition, but their sein could only slow down the ravages of time, not end them.

With Laghy babbling and crawling between them, it really didn't matter. Canumon pulled his wife and son closer to him to ward off reality a little longer.

It couldn't last. By the time soldiers pounded on their door, he was dressed in his combat robes and had finished his meditation. If all went according to schedule, he wouldn't fight Anyinn or any other human that day, but the schedule might no longer be relevant. They'd delayed any conflict with their status as warriors, but now far greater masters might seize hold of events.

"They've demanded a meeting," Kanavakis said as soon as Canumon got close. "Their champion can't possibly match a Zeitai, but they're projecting confidence."

"What's the plan, Kaen?"

"I have no idea. We stay back and await the Zeitai's orders. If another of those insane humans appears, don't hesitate to bring him down before he can interfere. But if he acts like these rumors, capture him alive so that the Zeitai can pass judgment."

Zeitai Terza was far from Laen Karnak and had no real jurisdiction, but Canumon kept his thoughts to himself. What mattered was that the Zeitai had power and the willingness to use it. That was the same reason he had little hope that the humans had found a champion simply to even the scales.

They had power. They would use it.

Both sides met at a great marble diamond beside the lodge, not so different from the Lonely Diamond where he'd fought Anyinn. Not so long ago, and in another sense very long indeed. On their side, the soldiers mostly maintained order, but he heard a few growls, and he could understand the sentiment behind them.

Across the diamond, the human crowd had shifted, eyes filled with a terrible passion. He fully understood them adamantly defending their land, but this was something different. Canumon searched for Anyinn and was relieved to find her sitting serenely, untouched by the rage of the others. Her Tranquil Blade piercing his sein would have been welcome at that moment, but the day wasn't really about them.

No, today their cause would be championed by the lone human man sitting cross-legged at one point of the diamond.

Though a few observers scorned the man known as the West Wind, everyone with any real sein training watched him closely. His pants and vest looked simple compared to Nolese robes, but his powerful frame sat with unnatural stillness. He had darker skin than humans in Nol, and instead of hair with pale highlights, pure raven locks flowed down his back. Though he didn't carry any apparent weapons, a band of willow sticks lay across his lap. That could be enough.

Then the Zeitai arrived, surrounded by his officers. He didn't step onto the marble floor and didn't even look at the human who had come to challenge him, instead focused on the Tayn clan across the diamond.

"My people requested to enter your land according to your own customs. Why are you bringing foreigners to challenge me?" He spoke in crisp Futhik and a moment later his words were translated by one of the four around him. Understanding both languages gave Canumon a strange sense of echoing, but the human crowds waited until the translator finished.

"That is our question for you." The human clan head, Feinouya, stepped forward to answer. "It is one thing for a Nolese Deathspawn to begin a challenge rite, but why have you come here? Your very presence is a threat."

A few of the soldiers growled at the slur, but the Zeitai's pale red eyes displayed no reaction whatsoever before he spoke. "I threaten no one, unless you have no legitimate reason for demanding my presence here. State it."

"By our laws..." The clan head hesitated and glanced back at someone Canumon couldn't see, though it wasn't Anyinn. "We are formally challenging your presence in the Taynol Valley, aside from the entry rite. For that reason, our representative will challenge you. Unless you successfully defend your right to stand here, you must depart our lands or face the Nolese Coalition."

The Zeitai growled and gestured to one of his officers. His brief command - "Humble the fool" - was not translated into Nolese, but many of the soldiers laughed.

One of the uniformed officers stepped into the arena and hefted a long spear. Its end carried a vicious point designed to pierce even the skin of warriors, but the officer took a reversed stance with the blunt end forward. Even that could be lethal in the right hands... though as the West Wind stood to his feet, Canumon doubted that he feared for his life.

When the blunt end of the spear thrust forward, the West Wind finally moved, deceptively languid. His willow stick met the spear head on, bent... and then somehow the spear tumbled into the air. In a single flowing movement, the West Wind stepped forward and brought the snapping stick against his opponent.

The officer toppled off the side of the marble at terrible speed, though he didn't appear to be injured. Everyone stared in shock as the spear tumbled end over end, eventually falling into the West Wind's free hand. He tossed it aside as he turned toward the Zeitai, then spoke.

"This is insult." His Nolese was rough with a barbarian accent, but Canumon doubted that the Zeitai even heard it. For him, the only real response had been the grace of the movements with the willow stick.

Waving aside his other officers, Zeitai Terza stepped onto the marble. For the first time, the West Wind smiled.

For a time, they simply stood and observed one another. Even the untrained soldiers hushed in anticipation, though they couldn't see that the match had already begun. Both masters extended themselves and analyzed their opponent with all of their senses, knowing the other's sein. Yet after that ended, they remained still a moment longer, their physical eyes meeting in the silence.

The two of them reached the center of the arena in a single step, exchanging techniques with cautious precision. Every one of the Zeitai's movements was traditional Laenan combat, polished to an impossible shine. His opponent moved with a fluidity that put most Nolese warriors to shame, yet followed none of their paths, his willow stick swishing faster than the wind.

Ferocious as the exchange was, it could almost have been mistaken for a simple brawl to someone without sein training. Both of them kept their feet planted and used only simple steps, and they countered everything thrown against them so effectively that no force escaped. While lesser masters might fight with great gusts of wind or shimmering sein, the two had such perfect control that they wasted no energy on demonstrations.

Canumon knew that he would have lost in the first few exchanges and could only watch in awe. It ended faster than he could follow, all he saw was that the Zeitai's palm struck the West Wind's chest and the human man dropped back a step.

Yet that had not been everything: though Canumon had missed the movements, one of the Zeitai's looping chains dangled from one end, sundered by the willow. Only when he raised a hand and touched his cheek did Canumon see the line of red tracing across it.

Both men smiled, and Canumon started to hope that they might not be within the deadly grip of this war. Yet when they stepped toward one another again, they had clearly decided that the time for games was over. Their next exchange ended swiftly, the West

Wind hurtling backward so swiftly that Canumon lost him completely.

His eyes needed to observe too many places at once. First he noted the Zeitai, eyes still focused without a hint of satisfaction. When he twisted his wrist, some of the silver chains in his uniform snapped around his arm, but Canumon couldn't understand the flow of his sein or how he used the chains. Beyond that, his eyes traced over the crowds, still recoiling from the explosion of wind.

Anyinn wasn't misled, instead tracking the West Wind in a different direction. The man had broken through one of the fortified stone pillars on a walkway and torn through the roof as well, shingles now raining down on the marble. But Anyinn was looking to the side... and there Canumon discovered the West Wind standing, apparently unharmed.

For a moment Canumon blandly observed that the West Wind was unusually durable for a human, despite his soft and pliable style. Then Canumon realized that this was no friendly demonstration and that foolishly staring at the fight put him in great danger.

One of the heavy shingles shattered against the marble, cracking it, but the Zeitai was already gone. The two met in an explosive burst, several more pieces of the walkway tearing free and scattering below. Panic set in on both sides and the crowds began to scramble to find cover.

Most were in position to retreat safely, so Canumon intended to join them, but at that moment something crashed into the side of one of the lodge's great multi-tiered buildings. One of the masters had thrown the other into it, but it scarcely mattered which was which.

The wood groaned like a wounded animal and then part of the building gave way, crashing down the side of the hill. Canumon realized that several soldiers and humans stood underneath, some oblivious and some staring in horror. If the dying building collapsed on them...

He crossed the space at a sprint, ducking another flying roof tile. When he arrived he simply grabbed whoever was closest and pulled them away... and in that moment felt a human's sein moving alongside him. Anyinn grabbed those nearest her, on both sides, and began pulling them to safety.

As they leapt away, she glanced over at him. They smiled at the strange parallel, but there was no time for words.

Though they managed to prevent anyone from being crushed by the collapse, the battle between the two masters still raged across the walkways of the lodge, threatening everyone below with a hail of debris. Canumon and Anyinn ducked behind a mossy boulder large enough to withstand the fragments and finally found space to speak over the crashing and screams.

"I could do that," Canumon said with a casual gesture toward the chaos, "but I have a cramp in my leg." He was gratified to see Anyinn's grim expression soften, if only for a moment.

"The two of them are going to tear the lodge apart." She kept her hand on the hilt of her sword, but there was clearly no point in drawing it. "I'm not sure we can survive either result."

"Even if we do, whichever one wins will have demonstrated a threat that will destroy any hope at negotiation. They might be fighting honorably now, but real concerns will take over once they finish."

Anyinn shook her head slowly. "The only way this could be any worse is if that insane hero joined them..."

As he heard her words, Canumon's eyes widened and he grinned, not caring how many teeth he showed. "Anyinn... would you like to go insane with me? These two ruffians have interrupted our appointed duel."

"But..." She paused as she realized what he truly meant, then shook her head again. Yet even as she did, he saw the steel in her eyes. "They've respected each other enough that I think it's worth the risk. Let's try."

With that, she lunged out from behind the boulder, and suddenly Canumon was committed to his mad idea. They couldn't move as swiftly as the two masters, but they could deflect pieces of debris and make their way to one of the central platforms. That alone was safe enough... the suicidal part was when they leapt up onto the walkway between the two masters.

"Stop this at once!" Anyinn called out. They weren't cut down immediately, so Canumon joined her.

"We have yet to duel to settle our differences. We cannot allow your battle to end ours."

The West Wind frowned, willow stick rising, but Anyinn spoke to him in a harsh tongue Canumon didn't know. When the West Wind replied, he spoke far more fluently than he had in Nolese, though Canumon still understood none of it. Which was just as well, because he needed all his attention for the Zeitai staring at him with burning eyes.

"Why bother with this ploy, Nin?" Zeitai Terza - the greatest warrior ever to come from the entire Laenan race, the supreme commander of their military - stepped forward without expression. Just staying on his feet was difficult enough, but Canumon forced himself to answer.

"I no longer serve, Zeitainan. The army hired me because they needed someone to earn their way into this valley by honorable combat. Whether or not my family finds a home may not matter to you, but it is everything to me."

For a moment he feared the Zeitai would strike him down, but eventually Terza opened his fist, letting the silver chains fall free. "This has become more important than you know. You're a bold man, so normally I would wish you well, but everything else is worthless compared to what's at stake."

"Then tell me the stakes. Tell me what you want, and if it's within my power, I'll find a way." For an old warrior to promise the Zeitai a boon was absurd, and Canumon saw a flicker of amusement on the Zeitai's face. But then his eyes became hard and shifted into the distance.

Toward a dark tent invisible in the mists.

"It doesn't matter what I want, but what he wants. This is the first time the Dark Lord has stirred in my lifetime."

The Dark Lord? Though Canumon might have sworn on his name on occasion, he wasn't sure that he truly believed in such a figure. The Zeitai were a fact of life, the exemplars of their factions and a driving force in the mansthein world. Believing in some shadowy master who stood behind them was impossible to accept, yet now it was his reality.

Behind him, the conversation between Anyinn and the West Wind continued. Canumon still couldn't understand their words, but the tenor suggested that they were not about to die. He took a deep breath and bowed to the Zeitai as low as he could.

"Zeitainan, please. Can his purposes be accomplished without war?"

"His purposes? No. But perhaps they do not require a war today." With that the Zeitai abruptly turned and stepped off the side of the walkway, dropping back toward the camp. Not long after, the West Wind made a final statement and then departed in the opposite direction.

Canumon collapsed like a marionette with its strings cut, and he found himself sitting on the cracked marble alongside Anyinn. Before they could catch their breath, both sides came to take them away.

Anyinn

Anyinn sat and stared at the page, as if by sheer force of will she could force it to reveal her own thoughts to her. Whenever she had a moment to sit down, she attempted to distill her thoughts into a form that would make sense to anyone who had not lived through the events. She might communicate a battle between masters - many plays and ballads did - but she could not bring herself to put words to the light and shadows that dominated her world.

Eventually her time withered and she set aside her quill in exchange for her sword. Their gambit had worked for the previous day, but there would be no more delaying: it was time to actually fight.

In all the turbulent uncertainty, Canumon stood firm as one piece of solid ground. With the Zeitai casting a shadow over everything and the mansthein man giving him an odd amount of respect, there had been moments when she doubted, but not any longer. They had fought and known one another's souls. That meant something that could not be denied by any story.

She left her room at the very hour the clan representatives came to escort her: robes in order, sword sharpened, sein prepared. Feinouya herself met her on the way, regarding her for a long moment before she finally nodded.

"You look ready. Whatever else you feel, you cannot hold back in this battle."

"I understand." Anyinn set aside the issue of what they would do, since she would have only a few moments with the clan head. "But what is our goal now? Do you think the mansthein will attack if they lose?"

"Winning or losing is less important than making everyone believe that your gambit yesterday was no mere ploy." Feinouya stopped and caught the hem of her robe, holding her in place. "Do you understand me, Anyinn? You don't need to cut off the

Deathspawn's head, but you need to fight him sincerely. We don't know how many will be watching."

Though Anyinn hesitated at the word, she decided to press on. "I thought this would be a mostly private fight."

"But the Deathspawn will have spies and the West Wind will be watching. Foreign savage... I'll admit he's strong, but I should have known better than to think he could take a role in Nolese politics..."

It seemed to Anyinn that they had left politics behind many days ago and now all played minor roles in some far worse game. She folded that thought away along with all the others and instead focused on honing her mind to a fine point. There were several potential directions their fight could go and she needed her full attention for all of them.

Instead of one of the grand dueling diamonds outside the lodge, they would fight in one of the chambers of the central building. Perhaps for the sake of privacy, or perhaps simply because their duel would not be impressive compared to the masters. Yet when Anyinn arrived, despite what Feinouya had said, there was a crowd of clan members on one side and mansthein on the other.

Canumon knelt in front of them, his hands calmly on his knees. She wanted to catch his eye and give some final indication as to what they would do, but he was a statue. Perhaps they would simply have an honest fight and that would be the end of it.

It began with less fanfare than any of their previous duels, barely even the traditional chimes. Anyinn drew her sword and set it in position, watching as Canumon rose and placed his feet in a familiar pattern.

She needed to resist the urge to smile as they began to move as they had so many times before. Though it was their familiar pattern, this time they held nothing back, each striking out with blows that could easily have been fatal. The familiarity made it easier for her to strike relentlessly, and the very aggression in their movements made it simple to avoid serious injury. Though anyone watching would have believed it was a fight for their lives, it was no different than their usual pattern.

Surging Leviathan. Waterfall Cascading Upward. Punishing Willow.

As always, she ended by manifesting her Tranquil Blade and driving it into his heart, but this time, Canumon copied her. The blade formed from his sein was not an exact copy, instead showing that he had deeply understood her technique and created something of his own. She wished that they had years to show one another the results of their lives, but the duel was over and the sein rushed through her.

His memory might not have been as pristine as her tranquil lake, but the emotions were overwhelmingly powerful. Anyinn completely lost her body and drowned in that night their families had shared together. Feeling it from his perspective made her cling to the foreign sein instead of casting it out, but in the end everything would return to equilibrium.

Opening her eyes, Anyinn saw the ceiling framed by a number of concerned faces. She weakly struggled to her feet, for the first time feeling the minor wounds she had taken throughout the fight. Even if they had avoided mortal blows, it was impossible to fight so passionately without trading injuries.

Most importantly, Canumon lay in a circle of his allies, apparently unconscious. She knew that he wasn't injured by her technique, so he must be prolonging the effect in order to make it look authentic. His sein had certainly taken a toll, given the concern she saw on the faces around her. Somehow her sword had fallen across the room and she sluggishly limped to pick it up.

"The duel is over, and the rite is concluded." Feinouya stepped between the two groups. "No territory is granted to any foreigners, but if he lives, Canumon will have earned the right to challenge for the territory at the border of the Taynol Valley. Further rites, especially by any other outsiders, must be negotiated on their own terms."

Not quite what they had hoped, but it was enough. Anyinn sagged back to the floor and let allied hands carry her deeper into the lodge. Since she had fought a duel for the clan and the head seemed pleased, she was immediately attended by healers, including an Estronese master. Even he could do little for the sein impact, and the healing left many deep aches, but by the time they concluded their work, her body felt mostly recovered.

"You've done your clan a great service," Feinouya said as she entered. With a wave of her hand, she dismissed everyone else in the chamber, then knelt down beside Anyinn. "If there is something you desire, I could try to grant it."

"I want... to rest." It wasn't what she had intended to say, but it was true. Anyinn considered changing her statement, yet there was something in the clan head's eyes that made her withhold her opinion.

"You would be an excellent warrior against the Deathspawn, but I respect that. Perhaps you and your family could be moved to one of our far-off holdings? There you could recuperate while the conflict with the Deathspawn becomes bloody."

"Why don't you call them the mansthein?"

Feinouya drew back, not in surprise but as if disappointed. "It doesn't matter what word they use for themselves, their identity has been made clear. So many generations have lived and died waiting for it, but now *we* live in the days of the Legend. I'm honored that our clan can take a role and that I can lead them in the battle against the Deathspawn."

"Do you hear what you're saying?" Anyinn forced herself up and caught Feinouya's sleeve, preventing her from leaving. "They outnumber us, and even a victory would cost us most of our students. You can't ask the Tayn clan to pay that price."

"Oh, but we volunteered."

Anyinn flinched as she heard the voice, her head involuntarily swiveling to the door. She knew who it was, yet she was still shocked to see Boulanu walk into the room. He was the brash young challenger she remembered, except that he was nothing like that man. Instead he carried himself with an agonizing self-importance that had nothing to do with youth.

"Boulanu has proved himself the Hero we've been waiting for." Feinouya escaped her limp fingers and walked to put her hands on the boy's shoulders. "He may be young, but he sees further than all of us. With our guidance, he will eradicate all the Deathspawn until only the Dark Lord remains."

"He's here." Boulanu took a deep breath and unleashed a disturbingly eager smile. "Lurking at the edges, causing all of this. If we kill him, we can end it all now."

"And the Tayn clan will be the saviors of all Nol."

"Of course. When the Legend called, you were the first to answer."

The cold dread gave way and Anyinn forced herself to her feet, glaring at the older woman. "Feinouya, do you really believe any of this? You saw the last man to call himself a Hero die for absolutely nothing, and he was twenty years Boulanu's senior."

"A madman." Though Feinouya sniffed as if the matter was insulting to even raise, a flicker of doubt passed through her eyes. Anyinn seized on it and stepped closer to the two of them, determined to break apart the certainty she saw growing between them.

"Enough." Boulanu raised a hand in her path and she actually stopped, despite her intentions. "I understand that you're angry because you weren't chosen to guide me. But all of that is in the past, long forgiven. You have played your part and you can leave the stage, if that is all you desire."

The surge of anger was an ugly and twisted thing, but Anyinn seized it, because it was the first emotion that had pierced the haze clouding her mind. Boulanu had been a reckless boy before and he was a reckless boy now, no matter what he called himself. Anyinn crafted a blade of sein to remind him of it.

Before she could strike, Feinouya caught her wrist and twisted her to the ground. Anyinn grimaced in pain, trying to will the shimmering blade into Boulanu, but her momentum had been broken. Even if she had been fresh, she couldn't defeat the clan head, so if Feinouya was serving as the boy's bodyguard...

"You see?" Boulanu turned and gave the clan head a saintly smile. "All things work for our good, in the end, and even she had her role to play. But come, we have a great deal to prepare."

And so they simply left her. With the healing chamber emptied, Anyinn sat completely alone, clinging to her memories of the conversation and trying to deny the sensation that she had failed.

All she could do was retreat to her chambers and try to write down what she had experienced, though the words rebelled against her. The glorious moment when Canumon had matched her own technique felt a lifetime ago. It seemed certain that Boulanu had been fundamentally changed in some way, yet thinking the idea meant nothing. This was no sein technique that she could counter, and if it existed as a mental phenomenon, it lay outside all her years of experience.

"Mother? Mother, are you there?"

Anyinn jolted from her despair and realized that she had been staring at the paper blankly. Impossible as it seemed, the voice was her daughter, calling from the door. An irrational impulse made her fear a trick until she wrenched the door open and found Heraenyas standing there, wearing traveling hat and robes with a sword in her hands.

Before her daughter could say another word, Anyinn swept down and embraced her. The girl squirmed, but for once she allowed her mother to hold her tightly. When Anyinn managed to force herself back, she kept her hands on the girl's shoulders, just staring at her as if the sight could erase everything else from that day.

"I... wanted to see your duel." Heraenyas gave her a broad smile. "I arrived too late, but I heard you won!"

"Heraenyas, why are you here?" Anyinn stared at the sword that had dug into her chest. "Where's your father? I can't believe he allowed this..." But even as she spoke, she realized that she had made the wrong assumption and her daughter squared her shoulders proudly.

"I sneaked out and came to help! There's going to be a battle against the Deathspawn, right?"

Horror and desperation nearly made Anyinn drive a blade of sein into her daughter's heart at that moment. But using such a powerful technique on a developing soul could have harmed her permanently, and in any case she wasn't sure that it would do any good. Instead she just stared at the light in her daughter's eyes.

"Mother? Why are you... is something wrong? I heard the Deathspawn attacked, but the Hero is here, right? If w-"

"No!" Anyinn gripped her daughter's shoulders so tightly that the girl whimpered. "Not you. Not... where did you hear these things?"

"Everyone is saying them!" Now staring at her in fear, Heraenyas clutched her sword more tightly. "I... I just wanted to help..."

"To help slaughter all the Deathspawn? Are you going to use that sword to cut off Laghy's head?"

Heraenyas let out a low moan and tried to wriggle away, but Anyinn refused to let her go. "No, I... not all of them... I don't want to kill anyone good..." Without warning she gave a cry and hurled the sword away, leaping into Anyinn's arms before it finished clattering on the floor.

Anyinn held her tightly and felt the girl's small arms squeezing her back with all the strength she had. Hot tears made their way down Anyinn's cheek, but for the first time she felt relief. The idea of losing her own daughter had been terrifying, but the blinding light had passed. A small part of her mind was disturbed that even young children could be susceptible to this curse, or that perhaps they were even more susceptible...

"I don't feel right." Heraenyas curled up against her, suddenly an even younger girl than she was. "I just wanted to help. My head feels all wrong..."

"We're leaving." Anyinn scooped her up and carried her out, leaving the sword where it lay on the floor. "Don't cry, Heraenyas. We're going to go home to your father. We'll eat together and sleep and then we can think about all of this."

The girl nodded, and though she stopped crying, she stayed curled up against Anyinn. Though she couldn't admit it, Anyinn was grateful to hold her daughter as she departed the Straedi lodge and began to run. She had thought the girl was forever too old for this, and though the circumstances were tragic, the fact that her daughter had come to her for comfort meant more than she could express.

With nothing to stop her, Anyinn sprinted as quickly as the girl could bear. The trip was still long, and soon enough Heraenyas grew weary and fell asleep against her. Anyinn held her tighter and used the time to think, the wind streaming past her clearing away some of the confusion that swarmed around her mind.

It was clear enough that running away was no solution. Canumon and his family remained at the lodge, and she could never leave them to the grandiose horror growing there. Only when that thought occurred to her did she begin to wonder if the madness went further than just the clan.

She had noted how the mansthein became angrier and restless, but what if that was not their true nature? It might be the presence of people calling themselves Heroes, or it might be the Zeitai... or the ominous figure in the dark tent. Though she had run too far, Anyinn still looked back over her shoulder as if she could see it. The corrupt story emanated from somewhere, and if she could find the source, perhaps she could end it.

But for the moment, she finished her sprint home. Heraenyas was still asleep, so Anyinn gently put her daughter to bed. In the morning they would talk to her and she would be kept as far away from the madness as possible.

The house seemed entirely empty, which troubled her until she found Noreinu in his study. He sat slumped in a chair, one hand stained with ink. A quill lay broken on his desk and several pieces of expensive paper had been crumpled up around him. She would have thought it was one of his creative moods, if not for the hollowness of his eyes.

"Anyinn..." He looked up at her as if he didn't quite believe it. "I thought... you were fighting today..."

"I did, but the duel doesn't matter." She sat down opposite him and leaned forward, taking his ink-stained hand and uncurling it from a fist. "Are you alright?"

"It's nothing. Just..." Noreinu sat back and shoved one of the crumpled papers with a bitter laugh. "I was trying to write a play and it was going poorly. You would have hated it. One of the war epics with rival clans, except I was going to rewrite the mansthein as one of the sides... the strokes were absurdly broad, but you know that plays well with crowds."

The familiar old complaint almost banished her fears... yet even that familiarity faded too soon. She rubbed his hand and spoke softly. "You've struggled to write before. What's different now?"

"Because it's useless. Every person on the damn street is only talking about one story these days, as if the Legend swallowed up everything else." He ran a hand through his graying hair and a beast of desperation lurked within his gaze. "Anything I want to write, it's already written, except worse and far more powerfully. I was thinking about it and I just felt so useless... I guess this seems trivial, doesn't it?"

"No." Anyinn leaned forward and wrapped her arms around his neck. "No, not at all. We need to talk."

"Are *you* well?" He pulled back enough to look at her, eyes penetrating. "I've never seen you so... what's wrong?"

"Perhaps everything, perhaps just me." She let them pull apart further, though she kept her hands on him. Noreinu would never let himself be swept up in such a blunt legend. "We need to go back to the lodge, before things get worse. But first, we need to visit the lake."

Canumon

Though Canumon awoke without any serious injuries, he woke in a different world. He had expected to find Kanavakis and other officers analyzing the exact details of their fight and perhaps condemning him for failing to win, since prolonging the stalemate might no longer be sufficient. Instead, he found himself alone in a complex that no longer seemed to care.

Slowly he realized that he had been returned to his chambers, which suggested that he hadn't been convicted and mansthein-human relationships hadn't turned to war. When he got up, he found the rooms eerily empty, and no soldiers guarded the exterior of the building. The entire lodge lay in a half-real state, the damage from the masters' battle cleaned up but the structures far from restored.

And throughout it all, the air closed on him like a hand around the throat. Anger and fear slid into his mind, almost as if he was under attack by foreign sein, yet his defenses were useless against it. He couldn't even tell himself that he was experiencing anything other than nerves, and yet...

"Canumon?" Gowanisa's voice made him spin with a flood of relief. She moved along one of the nearby walkways, bouncing Laghy in one arm. Their son was sucking on his fingers and looking around at everything with watery eyes, as if he had finished crying and was considering an encore.

"There you are." His voice sounded faint in his own ears and he rushed to them, wrapping his wife in his arms. Laghy squirmed into position between them and then flailed at his chest happily.

"Ca! Ca!"

All at once, the boy was perfectly content again, but after tickling his chin, Canumon had to look up at his wife. She was relieved to see him, but they both knew the reality of the situation couldn't be changed so easily. After a shared silence, she began to speak.

"The duel ended just like you wanted, but it doesn't matter. They haven't even begun any further negotiations for another challenge. No, don't ask - Anyinn is fine. The humans praised her and sent her to healers. But something is *wrong* over there, Canumon. There's this human calling himself the Hero..."

"Like the man who killed himself attacking the Zeitai's guards. It's a delusion unique to humans, I think."

"No. No, it isn't." Gowanisa pulled away and began walking along the rail by their rooms, bouncing Laghy absentmindedly to keep him happy. "This Hero is different. He's been preaching total war and everyone is listening, even though he's young. Just seeing him, from a distance... perhaps it really is like in the stories."

"Don't accept that." Canumon walked up behind her and leaned heavily on the rail, staring over the valley. "If we accept the terms of their Legend, we've already lost the battle."

"But you can't deny that something is happening. Don't you feel it in the air?"

"I do, but we can't respect it, can't let it be as grand as it believes itself to be." He rubbed his knuckles into his eyes roughly, trying to shake off the heavy atmosphere, then finally latched onto something. "There aren't multiple humans making these claims, always just one. And they do seem different. What if there really is something that passes between them? Could it be the sein shadow of some warrior driven to insanity?"

Gowanisa frowned skeptically, but considered it. "Can sein shadows pass between multiple people? You're the expert there, but that runs contrary to everything I've heard."

"That's a problem, I admit. Sein is life, and it can only linger temporarily over a strong connection. But it could be something similar, couldn't it?"

"What does it matter? If it convinces the humans to attack us..."

"It *matters*." Canumon brought a fist down on the railing, splintering the wood. Laghy stared in surprise, then clapped his hands together and chortled. "We have to think of this as a phenomenon we can understand, not a myth. If you let the enemy control the momentum..."

He trailed off, wondering what enemy he meant. Not humans in general, though the thought flickered in his mind for a heartbeat. It was impossible to fight an abstraction, yet it was those grand ideas that threatened him more than any weapon.

Before he could find any solution, tongues of flame leapt up in the valley below. His wife let out a low growl and rushed to the edge, peering closer as they realized that they might be too late.

Part of the camp was on fire and there were humans moving through it. No, they were attacking, striking down mansthein who tried to stand in their way. Some were beginning to regroup and fight back, but their organization faltered, leaving many to be struck down by the organized human force.

All of them rotated around a young man who walked forward without any weapon. For a moment Canumon saw a titan striding the earth, then a young human, then a pillar of white flame. He seized his own sein and made it still, forcing himself to look with his eyes instead of his heart.

They were led by a young man, not so many years past human adolescence. Something *was* different about him, even setting aside all potential illusions. If nothing else, older and stronger humans moved as he directed without the slightest hesitation.

"Zeitai!" The Hero's voice thundered over the valley, as if he possessed the sein of a far older warrior. "The Hero has come to end your life! How long will you hide yourself away?"

There was no answer from the emerald tent, not even a rustle of movement. Canumon looked back and found that Laghy was holding his ears and trying to burrow into his wife's armpit. She shook her head grimly. "The Zeitai went to consult with... whoever is in that black tent separated from all the others."

Canumon immediately turned to look, sein flowing to let his eyes pierce the mists to the peak beyond. The dark tent sat as quiet as the others. It lay some distance away, but for a master like the Zeitai, that space would be little obstacle. And yet there was no response, as if they had been abandoned to the madness of the humans.

Below, the Hero and his allies continued to slaughter their way into camp, but as the support staff and poorly trained soldiers fled, their progress slowed. Veterans formed a wall of pikes that proved difficult for the martial artists, and Catai began to form up. Their overgrown musculature and tough skin provided some resistance to any Nolese art, stopping the advance. Yet when they attempted to penetrate to the center, to reach the Hero, the humans fought back with renewed passion.

"We have to run." Canumon turned to his wife and grabbed her shoulders, dragging her focus away from the battle. "Take Laghy and go. As far away from here as possible."

"I'm not leaving you," Gowanisa insisted. "You can't be thinking of going down there?"

"That would be suicide. But I need to find Anyinn. We can't stop this battle, but if we don't create some way to contact each other..."

His wife stared at him for a moment, then abruptly turned and rushed back into their chambers to gather supplies. Canumon wondered if they even had time for that, given the fervor of the battle below. Even watching from a distance, he felt a rage rising within him, his heart pounding with every beat urging him to kill.

So long as the battle continued to stall, they had time. Yet at that moment, he saw the circling human defenses falter. One Catai managed to vault over several of them and he brought his axe down, striking the skull of the human Hero with a sickening sound.

His body fell and the axe fell with it, the Catai staggering back. Canumon's heart shuddered without understanding the reason and it took all his discipline to control himself. Below, he saw both sides hesitate, as if they all held the same breath...

Anyinn

Anyinn and Noreinu made their way back carefully, keeping to the pace her husband could maintain. She could have run home swiftly, but ever since visiting the lake, speed felt like a mistake. Her mind conjured scenarios that would require her to arrive as quickly as possible, yet she felt that rushing was a trap, falling into the rhythm of an unseen opponent.

The lake hadn't been the scene she remembered it, of course. Some trees had fallen and new ones had grown in their place, and the season was wrong for the falling leaves and dappled sunlight. Just sitting there with her husband and talking over everything that had happened still helped her to center herself and remain calm. If she encountered someone else claiming to be a Hero, she would not allow herself to be taken in.

Heraenyas remained at home with the servants, chastened and hopefully safe. Though Anyinn considered that it would be safer for Noreinu to remain back as well, she couldn't be certain that they would face a battle. If the conflict required negotiation or politics, she wanted him alongside her to keep her balanced.

They had discussed whether or not they should send clan messengers to contact their sons, and though she understood why Noreinu might want them there, she feared for them. To draw even more people into this maelstrom would only intensify it, and after so many steps had been taken in the wrong direction, she could not allow more.

Between one step and the next, Anyinn left the Taynol Valley and fell into a city of gold.

She felt a surreal power attempt to take hold of her and she could have sealed her mind against it, but instead she followed her first instinct and redirected it like a blow, moving along with the force. Her sight was consumed by a vision that she knew must be false, yet it screamed its reality to her mind.

Without having moved, she stood in the center of a vast city. She had thought it gold at first, but now she realized that only the sky was gold, the towering buildings instead formed from pale white stone. They rose skyward, shaped like the greatest of Nolese cities and yet empty. All around her they spread in neat patterns unlike any real city, desolate perfection.

Something stood behind her, she realized, with an awareness that had nothing to do with any of her combat experience. Anyinn turned calmly and found herself staring at a glowing outline. Though the glow was too bright to see any details, it stood at exactly her height and build, like a mirror image. When she took a step to the side to examine it, the glowing figure did not move.

"So much suffering..." If the figure had opened its mouth, it was impossible to see, but she heard the voice echoing in her own mind. "The story should flow toward its appointed ending, and yet all those who seek to carry it bring only pain and bloodshed."

"Who are you?" Anyinn asked, almost against her will.

"You ask that question to yourself, and it is the right question." Through the blinding light, she could just see the figure shift upward to stare toward the golden sky. "Are you the Hero who will lead your people through this chaos? Children and fools take the mantle without the wisdom to use it."

"Are you responsible for this? You... did you possess Boulanu?"

"You misunderstand. I am you, as you could be. He saw something within himself, but he failed to understand it, and so he was not truly the Hero. But one must arise, and so the suffering will continue until someone masters the challenge and tells a more peaceful tale. Is that you?"

Anyinn took a deep, shuddering breath, the air itself dead and golden. "You ask as if I have a choice."

"If you do not accept what you could be, another will. Perhaps it will be Feinouya, since she has desired power for so long. Then she would be able to eradicate the Deathspawn who threaten her clan."

"No. If... if I accept, will I be able to stop the fighting?"

"You will be able to do whatever you desire."

The words rang with falsehood, and she knew it was a lie that she was telling herself, yet Anyinn accepted it. Standing in that bleached white city, she knew with absolute certainty that the madness would only continue. It would claim the lives of young men like Boulanu, who could have grown into a good man if only she had served him better. Taking the power was wrong, but if she could save anyone...

Within the brilliant face, she thought she saw an even brighter smile, and then suddenly she found herself finishing her step in the Taynol Valley.

"Anyinn?" Noreinu turned back to her, only a slight frown on his face. "Is everything alright?"

"I just..." She stared down at her fingers, wondering what she saw. "Did something happen?"

"You stumbled for a moment. Since you haven't really stumbled in years, I wondered... are your injuries not fully healed?"

She had expected to find some golden horror clawing its way through her soul, yet Anyinn felt unchanged. There was nothing new in her sein or her mind, nothing like the strange light she remembered from the other Heroes. Her husband watched her in simple concern, in no way overwhelmed by her presence. Had it all been a moment of delusion?

Even if it was a whim, she decided that the threat of violence at the lodge was too great. Perhaps the entire vision had been her mind trying to warn her that Boulanu and Feinouya might cause deaths with their zealous fervor. Leaving Canumon and his family in such a dangerous place now seemed like the height of irresponsibility, though she remembered her desperate confusion at the time. Regardless of her experience, she was thinking clearly enough to know that she needed to act.

"Noreinu, I have a bad feeling about the lodge." She leaned in to kiss him briefly and smiled. "Follow me cautiously. I'll scout ahead and meet you before you arrive."

He agreed, though he was obviously troubled. Anyinn swept away from him, her robes flapping violently as she pressed through the wall of wind. Whether or not she was hallucinating golden encounters, the sensation that something terrible was about to happen intensified within her.

In shockingly little time, she reached the lodge and saw that her fears had been justified: bodies sprawled over the landscape beside the army camp. A righteous anger filled her as she looked over the human and mansthein bodies, none of which needed to die. Their lives had been spent on a meaningless conflict, a squabble over clan pride and the schemes of elites.

Even now, the two sides prepared to tear into one another. They had retreated from the first outbreak of violence, only to decide that they wanted another. Human warriors shouting retribution on one side, mansthein growling on the other... Anyinn raced between the two and raised her hands.

"Enough!" She called out as loudly as she could, expecting to have to shout over others, yet everyone turned to her in shock. Though the effectiveness of her shout surprised her as well, Anyinn found that she had enough words to continue. "This battle is over. All of you... go back home."

"You expect us to just obey you?" A monstrous Catai advanced, hefting a war hammer larger than her head. "You humans attacked us, for no reason, and we just defended ourselves!"

"If true, that attack is a crime we must apologize for. But more violence today will bring no one any justice. Turn back."

He let out an animal growl and lunged toward her, war hammer spinning in an overhead swing meant to cave in her head. Anyinn easily stepped aside from the broad movement, her sword singing from its sheath, lashing out to end the Deathspawn before he could rile up any of the others...

Anyinn's blade stopped just beside his neck, her entire arm trembling from the effort. Both of them stared at the edge, and it seemed that every eye in the valley watched her, but she slowly lowered her sword. Since the Catai still loomed over her, she didn't sheath it, but she instead tapped the point against his chest.

"I said turn back. The battle is over."

The enormous mansthein looked down into her eyes... and quailed. He shifted his grip on his hammer, as if his palms were slippery, and then suddenly turned and ran. As soon as he did, all the other mansthein joined him, terror in their eyes. They abandoned the destroyed part of their camp and even much of the rest, only regrouping when they reached the Zeitai's tent.

That retreat opened up an empty space between the two sides, and given their fear, another attack seemed unlikely. Anyinn stared at them, wondering at their terror. She felt no different, and for a moment she had been glad that they had finally listened to her calls for peace, yet something was wrong. Her sein flowed smoothly and peacefully, without disruption, yet...

"What are you doing, Anyinn?" Feinouya advanced on her, wildly gesturing toward the mansthein. "The Zeitai is gone! We have the chance to finish them now!"

As she always had been, the clan head was petty and vicious. It would have been better for both sides if she was removed... Anyinn carefully returned her sword to its sheath. "No. No more fighting. We should retreat and bury our dead."

Though the gathered clan warriors should have waited for a command from Feinouya, instead they began shuffling to obey. When she first arrived, their faces had been awash in shock and anger, but now she saw grief taking hold. So many lay dead around them... Anyinn placed her hand on the hilt of her sword, wondering if she could have done more.

With peace established, she turned toward the other side, just in case they intended an assault. They seemed intent on their own dead and wounded, but something lurked within the command pavilion. No doubt the Zeitai, or the power behind him in the dark tent, had intentionally avoided this battle. Some scheme brewed beneath the surface, and if she didn't uncover it, far more would suffer.

As Anyinn started to take a step, her eyes happened to slide upward and chanced upon Canumon and his family standing on a walkway. They stared down at her, and though she could see their faces clearly, she couldn't understand their expressions.

Stepping back, Anyinn forcibly turned away from the Zeitai's tent. A heartbeat ago, advancing to interrogate him had seemed entirely logical, and even now she feared that the next surge of violence might erupt from his shadow. His very presence had incited the mansthein, after all, and it was his threat that stopped the initial challenge rite that now felt almost quaint.

Unable to think clearly, Anyinn forced herself to move. She wanted to run back to her husband, or meet Canumon's family, yet both felt like the wrong step, not with her thoughts so light. Whatever she did, she needed to prevent more deaths, while the world still listened to her.

Looking past the human side of the aftermath, she saw a lone figure standing atop a small hill. The West Wind watched her and her alone, dark eyes absorbing everything. Before she could rethink her decision, or even make a decision at all, Anyinn leapt to meet him.

When she arrived, he simply stepped back to give her space, though she noted how he held the willow stick at his side. For a long time he stared directly into her eyes, his own a depthless ochre. It almost seemed as if he could see through all of her to some deeper essence, and when he glanced away, Anyinn let out a heavy breath.

"Do you understand what's happening here?" She asked the question in Coran, which felt crude compared to her own tongue.

"I have journeyed to many lands and encountered many warriors." The West Wind turned from her and stared out over the valley, tapping his willow stick against his leg. "I have seen more things than I believed possible. But this is something that I have never seen before. I must go to find answers, though I do not know if any exist."

"Wait. Please. Something's changed about me, hasn't it? The power has... passed to me."

"Not power, authority." As the West Wind stared into her eyes again, she remembered that Coran was also his second language. She wondered what he might say to her if he could express his thoughts fully, but his thoughts remained submerged beneath that placid gaze. "There were others like you, though everyone else has already forgotten. They believe... their lives can contain only one story. And now you are that story. Perhaps it is up to you what you write, but perhaps not."

With that, the West Wind stepped away, his mastery of sein carrying him from her in a blur that might as well have been the wind itself. This time, she did not think that he would return. That might have been the correct decision, yet she couldn't bring herself to leave.

The truce held between both sides, so Anyinn should have been happy. When Noreinu arrived much later, she clung to him fiercely.

Canumon

Negotiations began without warriors, by design. Everyone capable of using sein or even carrying a weapon retreated to their separate camps, while the central building of the lodge filled with mansthein and human diplomats. Or, in the absence of real diplomats, whatever family members, merchants, and support officers had enough authority to speak on anyone's behalf.

That left Canumon sitting outside and again unable to act, despite the fact that the negotiation technically still rested on his duel against Anyinn. Ironic that the meaning of the battle would be decided by those who had never fought in one, or perhaps appropriate. The rite was a pathetically thin justification for peace, after all the bloodshed, but Anyinn had forced it through.

He wasn't entirely sure what to make of her now, and she seemed to be avoiding him since the confrontation in which she had split the two sides. The crisis might be past, but his wife agreed that it changed nothing about the risk. While Gowanisa finished packing supplies for a journey, he bounced Laghy on one knee. The boy giggled and squirmed wildly, in defiance of everything around them.

"Do you want me to bring neth?" Gowanisa asked, leaning in from the other room. He only shook his head.

"I have a feeling we wouldn't have time to brew any."

"Right. I just... I think I have everything, but no matter what, I don't feel prepared." She walked closer, putting one hand on his shoulder and another on Laghy's head. The boy giggled and twisted to bite her fingers, but it wasn't enough to improve their mood.

"Do you have enough herbs?" Canumon asked. His wife slid her hand from his shoulder to rest on her stomach and closed her eyes. He wasn't sure if he could see a difference or if it was only hope. "You can throw out other things if you need more space."

"The problem isn't space, it's that we don't have enough." She sank down beside him, still rubbing Laghy's head. "I thought I could buy more from the army, but they're lacking most supplies beyond the basics. Everything we have will last me eight days, or sixteen if I stretch. So it all depends on whether or not we can reach a city with mansthein traders."

That seemed an open question, but before Canumon could answer someone rapped on the door. He leapt to his feet, his hands automatically shifting to a defensive position. Gowanisa snatched Laghy off his lap and the boy just squealed at what he thought was a game. There were no sounds of violence and Canumon felt no particular sein outside, but he still opened the door hesitantly.

Anyinn stood on the other side, holding a steaming kettle, which she offered with a weak smile. "My husband is busy with the other negotiators. Care for a cup of neth?"

"Why don't you come in?" Canumon smiled at her automatically, but his body failed to open the door as quickly as it should have while he stared at her.

In every physical respect, she looked unchanged, yet his deepest instincts told him that something had shifted. He felt as though his very senses were inadequate, like he watched the waves on the ocean and tried to divine the movements of beasts swimming deep below.

When Anyinn entered, she smiled at Gowanisa... and Laghy let out a cry. Suddenly bawling, he buried his head in his mother's chest and wailed in panic. Everyone stared uncomfortably before Gowanisa picked the boy up and carried him back to his room. Canumon tried to put out of mind the fact that it was the first time he remembered Laghy reacting poorly to anyone.

"I'm sorry, I didn't bring any cups." Anyinn sat down near the stove and kept her hand on the kettle. Canumon waved aside the issue and looked through the cabinet for the porcelain cups they'd used in that meeting that felt like ages ago. He started with a pair, then decided to take a third as well.

"I could use a good cup," he admitted as he sat down opposite her. Anyinn poured his neth first, her own, and a third after a slight hesitation.

"These cups are quite beautiful." She paused to admire the patterns around the side before she took her first sip. "They don't look like anything a local clan would make, so I take it you brought them with you?"

"The pattern is a traditional Laenan one, but I bought them in our own village, here in Nol." Canumon took a sip even though the neth was still too hot, letting it burn down his throat. "Back in Laen Karnak, they drink from cups like saucers, usually fashioned in squares."

"Squares? That seems like it would be prone to spilling."

"There's a channel to each corner. That's only for those who can afford them, of course. Standard saucers are made as cheaply as possible."

"Ah."

Anyinn lapsed into silence and they drank quietly for a time. Despite everything, it was enough, at least for that moment.

When their cups ran empty, Canumon reached to refill them, then hesitated. Instead he turned the empty cup over in his hands while he asked the question on his mind. "Out there, they all listened to you."

"I think the madness is inside me now." Anyinn took a deep breath and stared at her hand, slowly flexing each finger. "I had a... a vision I can't quite describe. But now, everything is different. Maybe I can define what this story means now, use it for peace instead of war."

"No." Canumon leaned forward, capturing her gaze. "You can't, Anyinn. Laghy knows you, he let you hold him at your home, but he cried when he saw you now. Whatever this is, I don't think any of us is in control."

"But I can carry it in another direction. Better my burden to bear than someone younger who migh-"

"Then treat it like a burden. If you really have this power, don't use it."

"Maybe you're right." Anyinn finally sat back and something of the intensity faded from her face. She lazily poured both of them a second cup and then stared out the window. "I don't feel any different. More confident, maybe, but I've always been confident."

Canumon frowned and tried to probe her soul as best he could. "You don't feel a difference in your sein? I admit that I don't, but I thought it would have to create one, if whatever this is has an impact."

"Well, maybe it's like you said, and we don't really know what we're talking about." She smiled at him and he smiled back, but they said nothing else.

Gowanisa emerged from the other room, a troubled expression on her face. Though she relaxed slightly when she saw their smiles, she didn't join them, instead lingering on the opposite side of the room. Canumon gestured to the remaining cup on the stove.

"We saved you a cup of neth so that you could savor it."

"I'm very grateful." She picked up the cup and immediately hurled the contents out the window before setting it back down. "Pour me another and I'll put it where it belongs too."

Despite the tension, or perhaps because of it, all of them laughed. Briefly. The pressure lifted from the room, but their problems ran deeper than any temporary stress. Anyinn drank some more neth and stared at the cup for a time before she set it down heavily.

"Thank you, both of you." She slowly rose to her feet and stepped toward the door, then hesitated. "I feel more myself, having spent time with you, but I think I need some time with myself now."

"Of course. Tell me if you learn anything." Canumon stepped forward to embrace her briefly, and after a pause, Gowanisa did as well. The two women shared a few whispered words he took care not to overhear, then Anyinn finally departed.

As soon as she was gone, Gowanisa marched back to the other room and hefted her pack onto one shoulder. "We need to leave."

"Because of that?" Canumon asked. "Surely you can trust Anyinn. You know her."

"I know Anyinn. Was that who was just here?" Her eyes burned defiantly, and though he disagreed, he couldn't find the words to do it.

When Canumon opened the door, he saw Anyinn vanish into the hills north of the lodge. Hopefully she would find some insight there, or at least the strength to resist the light burning inside her. If she became another Hero, as terrible as the others, he wasn't sure if he could fight her. In some way, he felt that it would be his duty to do so.

Gowanisa didn't press the matter, but resolutely continued to pack several final items. From the other room, Laghy began to cry again, desperate for their attention. This time, Canumon ignored him, all his attention consumed by a movement from the southern camp.

Kanavakis marched at the head of a column studded by Catai, armed and advancing toward the lodge. The warmth of the neth that had lingered within him vanished. He pushed the door open and turned back to Gowanisa.

"You were right. Run. Now." As he heard her move, he ran to intercept the mansthein soldiers.

Anyinn

It had been years since Anyinn had needed to meditate on specific memories, yet as she drifted into her sein, she found herself clinging to details. The further back she remembered, the more her mind was dominated by a pale haze. Unless she gripped them tightly, facts twisted out of her grasp and became seductively simple stories. Yet even those she held tightly...

Then, with a certainty that horrified her, she knew that the Deathspawn were attacking. The carefully gathered memories of her time with Canumon and Gowanisa made her shrink back from the word, but that didn't mean her impulse was wrong.

In a flash she was on her feet and running back to the Straedi lodge. For all the importance that had been placed on it, the complex wasn't so large. Sprinting down a hill toward it, she soon saw that the conflict spawned the only place it could:

outside the doors to the negotiation chamber. She could see Deathspawn soldiers there, including several Catai.

Two of the Deathspawn held Canumon prisoner, bound in chains, so she raced to his defense first. Several lay nearby, nursing broken arms, so he must have fought them first, but unsuccessfully. Rage flowed through Anyinn and she drew her sword as she reached the enemy.

Just before her blade connected, she redirected the edge and instead struck the man in the side of the head with the flat of her blade. She couldn't allow herself to think about that fact or fall into the simple rage: her goal was to rescue Canumon and nothing else.

Though the Catai should have had more time to react, they were so shocked by her appearance that she managed to strike down the entire group of them with non-lethal blows. Canumon dropped to one knee, staring at her in similar shock, then he abruptly shook his head and pointed inward.

"Anyinn... inside, you have to..."

She turned and pushed aside another of the mansthein, but there was only time to witness. Instead of a coherent scene, she saw only fragments: spatters of blood, broken tables, axes entering bodies already dead. Without fully understanding, she stepped inside, her body trembling except for her sword arm, which remained utterly still.

Of course she saw his body. She had known that she would. Noreinu didn't lie sprawled across the floor or over one of the desks, he slumped against the door to one of the other exits, as if he had died helping others escape. A long time ago, she had met him holding the door open for a group of elderly clan members, smiling kindly and so very young.

Before she realized it, Anyinn had grasped one of the Deathspawn by the head and brought his skull against a stone pillars. It cracked first, but she pulled him back and struck again.

Only as she resolutely bashed the man's head into the pillar did she start to feel any rage.

In fact, there was only rage. She watched her body as if from a great distance, aware of her anger without sensing it. Shouldn't she have been weeping for the loss of her husband of so many years? Instead, her eyes burned with something that made every Deathspawn soldier retreat from her.

Except one, who grabbed her by the arm. Anyinn nearly skewered him with her dangling sword before she realized that it was Canumon. She glared at him, yet he didn't flinch, unlike all the others. Slowly Anyinn disengaged, letting go of the bleeding skull.

She had grabbed one of the Catai, and his durable skull had survived the impacts, but with a slightly different decision she would have killed someone. That fact seemed like a simple error to her, something that needed to be corrected. But no, Canumon was right. If she wanted to bring justice to all the Deathspawn who had done this, murdering them herself would not be enough.

"Anyinn, you need to stay in control." Though they were surrounded by soldiers, Canumon was staring at her as if she was the greatest threat. "I know what they did, but if..."

"You're too late, human." One of the Deathspawn in a Laenan jacket stared at her with a revulsion she didn't understand and didn't care to understand. "Whatever you were planning to force on us, it's over."

"Kanavakis, don't." Canumon turned on him with the rage that Anyinn couldn't let herself feel. "You've killed your own people here, and for what? Were you ordered to do it?"

"What else could we do? Their 'Hero' had complete control of both sides, so I had to cut out the infection. But she left the defenseless-"

Stepping past the man's guards, Anyinn drove her sword through the Deathspawn. At the last moment she pierced his shoulder instead of his chest, but the momentum from her thrust drove them out of the room and across the walkway, scattering several other soldiers. Some had begun to flee, but her target struggled, pinned to the wall by her blade.

Abruptly Anyinn stepped back, staring at the terrified expression on his face. That should have meant something, yet she saw only the filthy Deathspawn who had killed her husband. It would have been justice to kill him then and there, and yet...

"I can't." She stepped back, letting go of her sword. "He deserves it, but if I do..."

"You're making the right choice, Anyinn." Canumon spoke softly, brushing her sleeve as he moved past her. "But you'll still have justice for Noreinu. Because I can."

If she had chosen to stop him, she could have moved with brilliant speed and exerted her will over them all. Instead, she turned away, barely seeing Canumon strike the Deathspawn leader's neck from the corner of her vision. To her surprise, she felt a chill roll through her instead of any satisfaction, as she should have been the one to kill him... Anyinn clung to that dissatisfaction and tried not to think.

When Canumon came to stand alongside her, he offered her sword hilt-first. He had taken the time to clean the blade, leaving it shimmering instead of covered in blood. She took a deep breath and accepted it from him, her fingers coming home around the hilt.

"Are we going to fight our way out?" Canumon asked. She realized that he was at her back and they were still surrounded by enemies. Once, she had wanted to fight together like this, except it had been an idle dream instead of a nightmare.

"All of you, go." Anyinn swept her blade at the remaining Deathspawn and watched them flee in terror, some tumbling down the hillside in their haste.

There was almost no one left alive in the lodge, except for the two of them. Her mind refused to reflect on that fact, but she could tell that Canumon was still thinking desperately. He looked back toward the chamber of corpses, covered his eyes, and then finally turned to her.

"This will mean war unless we stop it, get ahead of the story somehow. I suppose it all depends on what the Zeitai and the Dark Lord really want. Why haven't they appeared yet?"

"Because it isn't the proper time." Anyinn straightened her back and stared into the mountains. "Don't worry, Canumon. The story will be whatever we say that it is."

She had meant the words to comfort him, yet she saw an incomprehensible flicker of fear on his face. Considering that there might be some threat that she had missed, she turned back to listen to him, but he only stared at her for a long moment. Something higher in the hills caught his eye and he took a step forward.

"Gowanisa..." The sound of his wife's name sent Anyinn spinning, already sure of what she would see.

Part of the undefended Deathspawn camp had been taken by warriors of the Tayn clan, now herding together noncombatants. She could see the rage in their faces and several of them already lay dead, throats cut. Part of her thought that rage was good and right, while another part never saw them at all.

In the center of the group, Gowanisa fought back, but she was outnumbered and her opponents didn't hesitate to target Laghy in her arms. In the end Feinouya herself struck her arms, dislocating a shoulder. Gowanisa let out a cry of rage as her son fell to the ground, but there was nothing she could do against the clan head's overwhelming strength.

As soon as they had realized what they saw, both of them had started to run, but Anyinn knew that they would be too slow. When Feinouya tried to reach for Laghy, Gowanisa grabbed her leg and sank her teeth into it. Feinouya reacted with a vicious kick that sent her skidding over the ground, shielding her stomach. Immediately the clan head struck again, and Gowanisa barely managed to defend herself, the impact giving off a painful crack.

One of the other warriors pushed Laghy onto his back and lifted a spear overhead. Anyinn saw tears burning in the warrior's eyes and realized that he had likely just lost someone as well. It occurred to her as a dim, irrelevant fact that Feinouya's son had also been in the negotiation hall. That should have meant something to her, but it passed through her mind with little trace.

This time, she would not be too slow. She had already lost Noreinu and couldn't allow Canumon to feel that same pain. Anyinn rushed forward, denying the distance between them and crossing the distance in a glorious flash.

Her blade swept through the attacker cleanly, as if he didn't exist. Anyinn stared at the blood arcing from her sword with grim fascination, realizing the beauty of it.

"What are you doing?" Feinouya turned away from Gowanisa, staring at her in horror. "You... you're supposed to be the Hero! This is revenge for everything they took from u-"

Anyinn's blade found its way into her throat. The clan head stared at it in shock, having never believed that her savior would turn on her, but Anyinn was already losing interest. She would protect her friends, no matter who stood in her path. When the warriors around her stepped into her vision, she simply cut them down until there were none left.

They began to flee, as they should, but as Anyinn turned she saw more Deathspawn. The creatures were creeping around Gowanisa, no doubt intending to attack her. Anyinn struck first, defending Gowanisa from the woman lurking behind her. More people screamed around her and she heard them for only a moment before she put such thoughts out of mind. Their cries were making Gowanisa afraid, but she could remove them soon enough.

Canumon stood in her path and Anyinn frowned that he would turn against her. She struck out with a blinding slash... and somehow he deflected the sword. The abrupt failure made Anyinn stumble, hesitating for the first time since that beautiful arc of blood.

Though he attacked her and her soul screamed to cut him down, her body reacted automatically to the familiar movements. She realized that it was the sequence of techniques that had passed between them so many times and let herself fall into the response. As she did, she began to notice the terror on the faces of everyone around her.

Clearly, she had gone too far, though she struggled to remember why through the glorious light in her memory. Canumon would help her, that was her only hope. She knew him so well, every step and every strike, he would lead her back to the truth. If she followed the path they had forged together, she would find her way home.

Surging Leviathan. Waterfall Cascading Upward. Punishing Willow. And then her Tranquil Blade tore through his chest in a thrust of righteous light.

Canumon

As the pain forced its way through the shock, Canumon realized that he had failed. For a few steps, he had seen the old Anyinn again, not the Hero with flashing eyes striding out of Legend. When her sein cut into his heart, he saw the horror on her face. It made no difference to the mortal wound in his chest, but it mattered to him.

While he fell to the ground, Canumon took a deep breath and gathered all of the sein remaining within him. It was intended to be a final technique of desperation, allowing a warrior to fight beyond the limits of their body, but he had no intention of fighting. There had been enough violence that day.

From below, he saw Anyinn's empty hand shudder in horror and her sword dropping from the other. She fell beside him, trying to catch his body, but for once she was too slow. Instead she let out the scream of anguish that he had expected ever since she'd seen her husband's body.

Before he could rise, she manifested another blade of shimmering sein and drove it into her own chest. But this time, it didn't tear through her flesh, merely piercing her soul. She took a long, painful breath and then closed her eyes. After wiping them once, they remained dry.

With slow, methodical movements, Anyinn picked up her steel sword and raised it to her throat.

Canumon grasped her wrists with the last of his strength and forced the sword back down. Her dead eyes stared at him, briefly flickering with a futile little hope, but then her gaze shifted to his wound and the flow of his sein. She knew that he had already lost too much blood and that his body was sustained only by his last breaths of power. Despite all the ferocity she had displayed, her arms were weak as a child's.

"I know you're still there, Anyinn." Blood stained his lips as he spoke. "Don't let it end like this."

"Hasn't it ended?" Her hollow statement hurt worse than the blow to his chest, but he forced himself on.

"For me, but not for everyone else. Not for you."

"No, it's too late for me. And this is me." She raised her hands to her face, yet he couldn't tell if she was staring at them, or him, or something beyond both. "I thought it was some external spirit, but it isn't. This, part of this, has been within me all along."

"Why should that matter?" His words finally reached her and he saw her eyes - human eyes - finally meet his. "We haven't lost everything. We still have family left... if we let them die, then we truly will have lost ourselves. Anyinn, please..."

The next breath rasped painfully in his throat and he dropped. This time she caught him, guiding him onto his back. He strained to look past her, finding Gowanisa staring at them in shock and Laghy crying on the ground. For once, his wails were a blessed sound, because for all his sobs, he was still alive. Soon enough, Gowanisa drew him to her breast and his cries fell silent. Anyinn wiped her eyes again and retreated, so he reached a hand out to his wife.

She moved to him swiftly, lacing her claws through his. He could feel that several bones in her arms had broken, yet she still reached up to cradle the side of his face. Hot tears joined the blood covering his chest.

"Gowanisa... I forgive her, do you understand? This... this was always beyond us. We had... had..."

"I understand, you fool." She wiped her eyes roughly. "You were always a better person than I was."

"We fought as well as we could... not well enough, but we fought. You and Laghy have to live, or..."

His wife dropped her head against his shoulder and wept. Canumon could no longer feel his arms, yet saw one of them slowly rise at his command and touch her back. His entire body felt warm and cold at the same time, more peaceful than he expected as the last of his sein faded away.

"I never regretted being with you. Not for... not one heartbeat..."

Her hand clutched his as if she would never let go, but she needed to. Even his dying mind realized that more warriors remained on both sides, and the next slaughter might be the last. So Canumon let his hand grow slack, closed his eyes, and stilled his breathing. Gowanisa wept over him for a while longer, then forced herself away.

Once he heard their footsteps, Canumon opened his eyes one final time. His heart had stopped beating and he was nothing but a few whispers of sein in a corpse, but he could watch them. This time his eyes remained open as he saw his wife, his son, and his last friend disappear into the mists together.

Anyinn

Though Anyinn swung with the sword she had used for over a decade, it was no longer her familiar blade. Instead of a length of steel, it was a ray of light, the incarnation of terrible justice. All who stood before her were cut down, everything they might have believed simply denied by her strikes.

It was no rampage, she was making the world right. She swung with the old certainty that in her wisdom she knew better, and that the world should conform to what she knew to be true. Where she and Canumon had struggled to redefine the conflict, now she could change those stories and ignore the violence her targets had to offer. Only glances toward Gowanisa kept her in check, remembering how her wisdom had been wrong, but those memories dimmed with each moment as she tore a path back to the place that had once been home.

But it was no longer her home. That house had been occupied by a woman named Anyinn who no longer existed. When she had struck herself with the Tranquil Blade, the memory had glowed with new purpose that left no trace of her memory. A glorious sun burned down over the tree and transformed the lake into a blinding mirror in which she could see nothing.

Only a single purpose blazed inside her: the remnants of their families had to live. Beside her, Gowanisa kept pace despite her injuries and the look in her eyes. Laghy still sobbed whenever she looked in his direction, but his mother only stared back with bleak determination. Feeling her husband die in her arms had left her deadened beyond the terror that Anyinn wreaked on the world.

They left behind the growing violence and finally arrived at the small house. Her mind had expected a blood-covered battleground, yet it lay perversely untouched, as if there had been no deaths at all.

"Mother?" Heraenyas peeked from the door, staring at them with wide eyes. "Everyone else said something terrible had happened and left me. But you said to stay here, so I-"

Anyinn cut her off with an embrace at full speed, startling the girl. When she pulled back, she saw fear in her daughter's eyes, though not toward her. She wished that she would wipe it away, yet knew that such things were no longer within her power. Now she had only a single terrible certainty to give, nothing that a mother should have been able to offer.

"Mother? Why are you crying?"

"There's been a battle." The words fell dully from her lips and she had to close her eyes against her daughter's questing gaze. "I'm sorry, but your father is dead. Canumon died so that we could escape. You need to leave with Gowanisa now, or..."

"No!" Heraenyas leapt forward, clinging to her. "He's dead? I can't go! How? Can I stay with you? Please, I can't..."

"Heraenyas, you have to listen to me. Gowanisa's arms are injured, so she needs your help to take care of Laghy. You need to leave quickly, do you understand? People might come after you, and I need to stop them."

"And then you'll come after us, right?"

She had told herself that she wouldn't lie to her daughter. "Yes."

Gowanisa had dropped to the ground to let Laghy crawl on his own while she massaged her broken arm. When Anyinn turned toward her, the mansthein woman returned her flat gaze and slowly rose. They stepped away from the children, staring at one another in silence until Gowanisa finally spoke.

"You're really going to trust me with your daughter's life? I wouldn't."

"I'm not sure I know myself, but I think I still know you, Gowanisa." Anyinn wanted to smile and found nothing but terrible confidence welling up inside her. "I would say I'm sorry, but nothing I say can possibly..."

"Damn right. He might have forgiven you, but I won't."

They were interrupted by a sudden laugh, and both turned to find Laghy giggling. All Heraenyas had done was pull out a wooden toy, yet it delighted him endlessly. The girl still had tears in the corners of her eyes, and the boy would cry again, but for now, they were happy.

"She doesn't know how young she is," Anyinn said slowly. "What I've done to her, leaving like this... it isn't right. Perhaps I could have been a better mother, but it's too late now. When she's ready, you need to talk to her. To make sure this doesn't consume her."

Gowanisa heaved a deep breath. "You're really putting that on me?"

"It's all I have left."

For a time Gowanisa simply stared at her, red eyes glowing, and then she gave a strange smile. Despite all she had learned about mansthein smiles, Anyinn had no idea what it meant.

There were more words after that, and many preparations, but that was the end. Anyinn helped them gather whatever could be of any use in the house and sent them off on a path that would take them far from the Taynol Valley, hopefully to safety. The desire to go with them and slaughter anyone who might harm them smoldered inside her, but she knew that was the one choice she could no longer make.

Eventually they departed, Gowanisa leading Heraenyas, who held Laghy in her hands. As they dwindled in the distance, Heraenyas turned back and waved to her, as if they would see one another again soon. Anyinn wanted to give her a final farewell and instead merely waved back.

Then she was finally alone, as she should have been ever since she'd tasted the golden fire. She carefully cut off part of her robe and fixed it on the pole atop the house, the blue signaling a grave. After staring at it fluttering in the wind for a time, she dropped into the yard behind the house and said her last farewell.

The daughter she might have had was remembered now only by a single stone, unmarked except for her name. She had never taken a breath, all that she might have been coming to an early end, just as her relationship with Canumon's family had been choked by the purpose still coursing through her. But she had lived, and they had lived, and that emotion had meaning even if they were all forgotten.

Anyinn dropped her sword on the floor of the empty house, an utterly empty gesture: she knew that she would pick it up again soon. But for now, the pain eroded all the glorious purpose within her and she wandered through her old home as a ghost.

Memories faded through her mind, a painful warmth. Not just her grown children, but the four of them talking around the fire, Heraenyas and Laghy playing in front of the fire. She realized that she was making her way to her bedroom, where all her papers still lay scattered on the desk. Her manuscript was completely useless now, since she would be hated if she was remembered at all. The woman who had ended the Tayn clan... the only thing worse would be the savior of the clan.

Yet though she had nothing to give, Anyinn found herself sitting down. Her thoughts echoed with the terrible light in that fatal blow and how it had felt to drive her sein into herself. Trying to put the horrors of that day into words was a futile task, but in this one small thing, she could take back a tiny fragment of insight. She picked up her quill and began to write.

Postscript

The manuscript ends not with any information about the bloodiest day of those events, but with an apparent return to the simple technique descriptions of the beginning. It is possible that the events are encoded in some way, because the sein instructors I showed the manuscript said that the technique described in the final pages is incomprehensible.

The lack of closure again works against any illicit purpose a false document might desire - such techniques may have been in vogue in years past, but they hold little appeal to popular audiences. If it was intended to deceive, the deception must be aimed toward scholars attempting to discern the truth of the Legend. Given how this war is increasingly fought with the quill instead of any blade, this possibility cannot be discounted. I only hope that revealing this manuscript strikes at least a small blow for our Hero and in support of the one true Legend.

My attempts to track down the allegedly surviving members of either family have resulted in failure, though it is possible that they died in the subsequent chaos. My contact in the enemy military says that there is no record of the supposed operation in the valley or of any of the Deathspawn involved rejoining their legions.

Investigating the Taynol Valley itself proved difficult, as locals refused to enter, citing superstitious reasons. When I hired an outside agent, they claimed to find two unmarked graves at the site. Strangely, the manuscript offers us no explanation for this, so both the site and the document will perhaps remain a mystery.

The Hero

The Hero walked to the top of the mountain slowly, bearing the Deathspawn corpse in her arms. She knew that she needed to carry it, though it was easier not to think about why. At least no one else stood in her path, though the base of the mountain had been scattered with corpses.

Before her, she finally saw her destination: a tent formed from darkness itself.

"Come out, Dark Lord! I'm here to slay you!" The Hero laughed bitterly and set down the body. "I've killed a dear friend. That makes me a great Hero, doesn't it?"

A light within her had expected a glorious battle against her final foe, while a lingering piece of herself had wondered if the tent was entirely abandoned. She felt nothing within it and the dark canvas barely even moved in the wind. Perhaps they had all been driven to madness by an empty tent atop a mountain.

Finally he emerged, a monstrous Deathspawn who straightened to over twice her height. The darkness of his body made the tent look like mere gray, his maw of knives burned with infernal flames, and his eyes glowed like the father of all Deathspawn. Smiling to herself, the Hero put her hands on her hips.

"So you do exist. Are we going to fight now?"

"Fights occur between people, and we are no longer that." His voice was surprisingly soft for such a large being, resonant but not as deep as she had expected. When she looked into those pure crimson eyes, she saw not hatred, but an ancient weariness that engulfed her own. "Now we are but symbols."

"The two of us are the same, aren't we?" She stared up at him, understanding for the first time. "I've already lost so much of myself to this... role. How long have you been the Dark Lord?"

"A very long time." He moved ponderously, walking past her to sit down at the edge of a cliff. When she only stared, he patted the ground beside him. "Come and sit."

"But we *are* going to try to kill each other, aren't we?"

"Yes."

"And you'll win, won't you?"

His eyes met hers somberly and he hesitated, as if considering whether or not to lie. When he spoke, she remained uncertain of his decision. "Most likely. The time is not yet right for the Legend to take this course, so it will betray you one last time."

The Hero stared at him, the broken pieces that formed her at war, and then she slowly went to sit down beside him. To her surprise, the mists looked much fainter from the heights, letting her see over a vast swath of the Taynol Valley. She knew there must be fires and destruction spreading throughout, yet for the moment, it appeared tranquil.

"Did you order my husband's death?" she asked. There was no need for further detail, regardless of how much he understood of her question.

"I didn't, but does that really matter? My presence killed him nonetheless. It will not be the last, but I trust that there will one day be a final death."

She closed her eyes and concentrated on the wind moving past her, not trusting in hope. "If we killed one another, would it end?"

"No, I don't believe so." The Dark Lord shifted audibly and she opened her eyes to find him staring down at her with something new in his gaze. "But I am not willing to accept that outcome. You have seen what others have done with the power they were given. I must carry this role until the end, or there will be no end."

"And what end is that?"

He didn't answer for a long time, and when he spoke his voice was even softer. "Your home is beautiful. I will not say that I am sorry, but I do wish that it could have been different. If I had understood the consequences, or found some other way..."

"Is there anything more I can do? Not for myself, but for everyone left."

"By stepping off the path, you have already done all you can. For the first time I have witnessed, the light has receded into uncertainty, if only for a moment. The world will know another Hero, but not here, and not now. Perhaps in the Chorhan Expanse, or perhaps across the oceans. There, we might hope..."

"Hope is my domain, Dark Lord. Shouldn't you be talking about terror and destruction?"

The monstrous face split into an inhuman smile and the Hero felt that she sat alongside another person for the first time since she had lost all the others. She knew how it would end, yet she found herself reluctant to accept it. If she could have stared out over her home, surrounded by both her families, she would have been content. Only now, when it was beyond mattering, did she find herself here.

"Was I..." The Hero didn't want to ask the question, but she forced herself on. "Was I in control of myself, or am I in the grip of something else? Has it controlled me, or has some part of myself done all these things?"

"Would either answer make you feel less guilty?" the Dark Lord asked. It was no answer at all, and yet all the answer she needed.

"Can you spare the valley further violence? I don't care if you needed something here or if it was all lies... is it possible for you to lift any of the burden from them?"

"I will try."

"Then I suppose there is only one more thing to ask: can you bury the man I brought with me? He deserved better than I could give him. And, when we've played out our roles, can you bury me next to him?"

The Dark Lord nodded and she knew that he would keep his word, the first certainty that didn't leave her sickened in a long time. She breathed deeply of the mountain wind and stared out over the Taynol Valley one last time. Though it was no longer her home, it might be a home again.

The Hero lay back and Anyinn closed her eyes to rest.

X X X

Thank you for reading this novella! This was a story I simply wanted to write, so it's going out into the world without any real business plan. If you enjoyed it, it would mean a lot to me for you to leave a review.

Want to review this book?

BFS is a standalone novel that takes place in the world of my epic fantasy series, The Brightest Shadow. It's a different sort of beast, attempting to tackle similar themes from a very different angle and over a much larger canvas. If you're interested, you can begin reading here:

https://www.amazon.com/gp/product/B0856ZMG9Z/

And if you follow along for long enough, a few piece of this little novella might turn out to be more relevant than you'd expect. ^-^

Here are some other ways you can keep up with my work:

Patreon: https://www.patreon.com/sarahlin

Mailing List: http://eepurl.com/dMSw2A

Blog: http://sarahlinauthor.blogspot.com/

Facebook: https://www.facebook.com/Sarah-Lin-1041738042689736/

Acknowledgments

Thank you to all my alpha and beta readers for their feedback, particularly the septuagenarian squad for offering all their perspectives on older protagonists.

Thanks to Cultivation Novels, Western Cultivation, and GameLit Society for the community.

Made in the USA
Columbia, SC
09 December 2024